NEW WRITERS! NEW STORIES!
A NEW DIMENSION IN SCIENCE FICTION!

A demented captain navigates
a spaceship carrying frozen bodies.

A dying race searches desperately for food.

Archaeologists on an alien
planet uncover strange artifacts.

An exotic world of gentle
humanoids is menaced by a bizarre evil.

NEW WRITINGS IN S-F3

NEW WRITINGS IN
S·F3

EDITED BY JOHN CARNELL

NEW WRITINGS IN S-F3
A Bantam Book

PRINTING HISTORY
*Originally published in Great Britain
by Dobson Books, Ltd., 1965*
Corgi edition published 1965
Bantam edition published February 1967

Bantam Books are published by Bantam Books, Inc., a subsidiary
of Grosset & Dunlap, Inc. Its trade-mark, consisting of the words
"Bantam Books" and the portrayal of a bantam, is registered in the
United States Patent Office and in other countries. Marca Registrada.
Bantam Books, Inc., 271 Madison Avenue, New York, N.Y. 10016.

Contents

Foreword

In this third volume of *New Writings in S-F* we take a much wider cross-section of contemporary themes by present-day writers. All but one of the stories have never been published before—in fact most were written specially for this series. The sole exception, Frederik Pohl's "The Fiend", will not have been read by many regular S-F readers, as it originally appeared in *Playboy,* an American magazine with the broadest of broad policies devoted to masculine appeal.

The inclusion of the Pohl story was deliberate, in view of the many admirers of his own works (novels and short stories) and his brilliant collaborations with the late C. M. Kornbluth of satires exposing our own life and times against future backgrounds—*The Space Merchants, Gladiators-at-Law, Wolfbane,* etc. Here is a new type of Pohl story, written for a specific market, with all the trappings of S-F shifted slightly into a new angle.

At the other end of the scale, Colin Kapp's "The Subways of Tazoo" is one of the finest *science*-fiction stories for a long time, but here we have a science which is, at first, completely alien to Man. Few themes stir the imagination more than that of archaeological research, whether it be of ancient Egyptian or Roman remains or a Kon-Tiki expedition to prove a possibility. In science fiction, the quest is always for traces of another intelligence or artifacts left behind by people long departed. The Kapp story combines the best of these possibilities with the finding of an alien culture so different from our own that it is almost incomprehensible—but not quite; which makes the story.

Stories evolved round the mental powers (psi) have been particularly popular since the advent of space satellites, many authors feeling that with Man practically on the threshold of space travel it was time to turn the spotlight of literary research inward upon the mind itself. There have been many fine stories upon this subject and a great deal of rubbish.

John Kingston's "Manipulation" is obviously in the former class as he unfolds the suspenseful story of a man "gifted" with such a power he is not equipped to handle successfully.

There is a sharp change of pace and ideas in Keith Roberts's story "Boulter's Canaries", the background theme to which is a poltergeist (usually reserved for weird stories) but Mr. Roberts turns a scientific eye on this phenomena and finds a different answer to the one usually given by psychic research experts.

For those who like space stories, however, there are at least four different types in this collection, each with a moral to prove if you look at them in retrospect. Two vignettes—John Baxter's "Testament" and James Inglis's "Night Watch"—are so dissimilar that they might well be the alpha and omega of the collection, for in the former the main theme is one of a desperate search for food and water to prevent a race dying, and in the latter we see the end of the galaxy. In between these two extremes both Dan Morgan and James H. Schmitz present unusual themes in "Emreth" and "Spacemaster".

Basically, then, this is a new collection of stories designed primarily for enjoyment. That one or more of them will evoke speculation in some readers' minds is almost certain, for this has been the main feature of S-F for over fifty years. A sense of wonder and a sense of enjoyment go hand in hand. *New Writings in S-F3* should provide you with both.

JOHN CARNELL

NOVEMBER 1964

The Subways of Tazoo

by

COLIN KAPP

While archaeologists continue to unravel the mysteries of former civilizations on Earth, science-fiction writers have been speculating on the possibility that one day we may find similar traces of alien intelligence on other worlds—Mars, for instance. Author Colin Kapp, however, takes us further away, to an alien planet with a lost civilization and the incomprehensible artifacts they left behind in their flight from ...what?

ONE

"Lieutenant Van Noon, report to Colonel Belling's office."

"Damn!" Fritz Van Noon glared at the loudspeaker. "Sounds as though Belling's back and on the warpath again."

"Can you wonder?" Jacko Hine helped him out from under the miscellanea of half-assembled pieces. "Let's face it, Fritz, some of our recent projects have come unstuck in a rather spectacular manner."

"True," said Fritz, "but never let it be said that the Unorthodox Engineers have produced a damp squib. Always our results have exceeded our wildest expectations."

"Or Belling's wildest fears," said Jacko morosely.

As Fritz entered the office Colonel Belling half raised himself from his chair in greeting. "Ah, Van Noon! Just the fellow I wanted to see."

"Sir?" asked Fritz suspiciously. Colonel Belling was not a man given to cordiality towards his subordinates.

Belling smiled wolfishly. "I've just returned from the General Staff conference. Since you re-instated the railways up on Cannis even the Old Man has been forced to admit that there may be occasions when unorthodox engineering has its virtues. For my part I felt impelled to point out that I'm trying to run a specialist engineering reserve, and that carrying the can for a complete squad of engineering illegitimates was not strictly within my terms of reference. As I explained, always I get stuck with the one engineer in a thousand who should never have left kindergarten, let alone graduated. The only repository I have for these mechanical misfits is the U.E. squad, where the damage they can do, if not exactly nullified, is at least anticipated."

"Isn't that a little unfair, sir? I mean . . ."

"I know just what you mean, Fritz, and I don't accept it. Engineering is a discipline, but the brand you apply is strictly delinquent. The outcome of the conference was that Colonel Nash, whom I'm beginning to suspect has masochistic tendencies, has volunteered to take the U.E. squad on the Tazoon enterprise."

Fritz considered this for a moment. "Exactly what are they doing on Tazoo, sir?"

"Supporting an archaeological team. Life on Tazoo is now extinct, but evidence tends to show that it once held a civilization as highly developed or more so than our own. In terms of knowledge to be gained it is probably the greatest find that space has ever given to us. It is doubtful if the Tazoons were human or even humanoid, and they became extinct at least two million years ago. Our problem is to pick up the remains of a complex mechanical culture as alien and as old as that and attempt to understand it for what it was."

"I shouldn't have thought that was too difficult, sir."

"No, Fritz, I never supposed you would. That's partly the reason you're going. Your inverted-sideways approach is the nearest thing to an alien technology that we've got. That makes you a specialist."

"Thank you, sir," said Fritz warily. "And the other part of the reason we're going?"

"The climatic conditions on Tazoo are such hell that the average rugged ground-cat has a useful working life of about two weeks. That means the archaeologists can't explore enough from base to get at the really big finds they are certain exist. Fritz, I want you to provide them with transport to where they'll be most use—and if you don't, you'd better find another engineering reserve to come back to, because if you come back here . . ."

"I know," said Fritz unhappily, "you'll make me wish I'd opted to transfer my retirement pay to Tazoo."

"You know, Fritz," said Colonel Belling, "for a moment we reached a point of real understanding there. I think I'm going to rather enjoy the thoughts of you and the U.E. squad sweating it out in a hell-spot like Tazoo."

Touchdown on Tazoo. The transfer ferry had no viewports and afforded no opportunity for its passengers to receive a preview of their destination. Even the ground-cat which rendezvoused at the landing site close-coupled its hatches with the ferry's air lock before the transfer of passengers and goods began. In the cabin of the ground-cat, shutters likewise obscured the view and cheated Fritz of his moment of revelation.

"Allow me to introduce myself," said the cabin's occupant. "The name is Philip Nevill, Archaeologist in Charge."

"Van Noon," said Fritz. "Engineer extraordinary—and this is Jacko Hine, one of my staff."

Nevill grinned affably. "Your reputation preceded you, my boy. Frankly, when I heard of you I persuaded Colonel Nash to get you here at any cost. There are things on Tazoo it'll take a very liberal mind indeed to understand."

The ground-cat struggled away from the ferry, its engine coughing in asthmatic complaint.

"So I've heard," said Fritz. "Look, do you mind if I open the shutter for a second? I'd like to know the worst right from the start."

"Help yourself," said Nevill, "but I promise you it's a passion you'll soon lose."

Fritz fought the shutter from the window and peered out for his first glimpse of Tazoo. Heavy cloudbanks filtered the furious sunlight to a brilliant monochromatic red which hurt his eyes and rendered all colours as shades of red or the darkest, sooty black. The terrain itself was nothing but a lumpy, featureless waste as far as the eye could see.

"Satisfied?" asked Nevill.

Fritz dropped the shutter back with a clang and closed his eyes.

"Painful, isn't it?" asked Nevill. "Normal endurance is about forty minutes before red-blindness sets in. Very bad for the eyes, to say nothing of the psychological effects. Incidentally, the ultraviolet radiation for two hours after dawn and two hours before sunset is strong enough to take the skin off you in about three minutes flat."

"Charming!" said Fritz. "And what's it like at midday?"

Nevill raised his eyes to the ceiling. "Ruddy awful!" he said.

At the blare of the ground-cat's horn Nevill opened the shutter again. "There's the base—way over yonder."

Fritz scowled at the blood-red panorama. Perhaps half a kilometre away was the base, like a cluster of cherries half-submerged in a waste of pink icing.

"Underground, eh? A very sensible precaution."

"It isn't underground," said Nevill in a slightly aggrieved tone. "It's a surface installation."

"But I don't see anything but some almighty balls of mud."

"They're standard Knudsen huts with a protective skin on. There's a sandstorm that whips up every night which would sandblast an unprotected Knudsen to a skeleton before dawn. We spray each hut weekly with a highly plasticized poly-polymer which is reasonably abrasive resistant. The plastic traps some of the sand and this materially increases its resistance, but builds up and completely ruins the shape."

Abruptly the engine of the ground-cat coughed and died. Nevill held a rapid exchange over the intercom with the driver.

"Engine's gone," he said finally. "Either the carburettor's etched away or the damn sand has got into the cylinders— or both. Anyway, the cat is a write-off for all practical purposes, so there's nothing for it but to walk—and it's too near evening for that to be funny."

They descended from the cabin, Fritz and Jacko choking quietly in the acrid air which caught at their noses and made their lungs feel raw. Nevill, acclimatized, was surveying the sky anxiously. Above them the swirling cloudbanks, blood-red trailing into purple and black, plunged across the darkening sky so low that Fritz had an almost compulsive desire to put up his hands to see if he could touch them. There must have been a high wind above, for the cloudrace was certainly moving at better than a hundred kilometres an hour, yet on the ground the warm humidity was deathly still, as though a sheet of glass insulated them from the driving turbulence.

Nevill was worried. "Looks like a storm," he said.

"Is that bad?" asked Fritz.

"Only if you're unlucky enough to be out in it. Let's hope it's a wet storm. They're decidedly uncomfortable, but not usually fatal if you can get to shelter quickly enough."

"Why, what happens?"

"Nothing spectacular if you can find shelter from a hundred kilometre per hour damp sandstorm and if you happen to have sufficient alkali available to neutralize the rain on your skin."

"Neutralize the rain?" said Fritz, his voice rising. "What the blazes is in it?"

"Oh, about five per cent sulphuric acid plus a trace of hydrogen chloride with a little free ionized chlorine. Stings like hell, but it's better than a dry storm."

"I'll buy it," Fritz said helplessly. "If a wet sandstorm is equal to an accelerated metal descaling process, what's a dry storm equal to?"

By now Nevill was deeply concerned, scanning the furious cloudrace with worried and experienced eyes. They were still three hundred metres from the nearest part of the base, with Jacko and the driver close behind.

"I think you're going to have a practical demonstration of a dry storm, Fritz. If the smell of ozone becomes intolerable or if you hear anything like a bee buzzing don't hesitate —just drop to the ground as fast as you are able. If you can find a hollow then roll into it, otherwise don't bother —but whatever you do, be quick."

"A bee buzzing?"

"Air ionization path, the prelude to a lightning bolt. There's a few mega-megavolt not many metres up in the cloudrace, and it packs a current that can not only char a man but also fuse him very neatly into the sand. The carbon from the body reduces a great many metal oxides in the ground so that the resultant slag forms a remarkable range of glasses."

"Forget the chemistry," said Fritz hastily. "I never could see myself making a very convincing paperweight."

"Then drop!" said Nevill, suiting action to the words.

They all dropped to the ground. Fritz's nose didn't have time to detect the ozone, virtually paralysed as it was by the existing acridity, but his ears did register the sudden buzz which Nevill had anticipated by a half second. Then the lightning bolt, a blaze of vivid energy a mere thirty metres distant, spat like a column of angry fire rising to the heavens. The noise and the shock-wave of its passing stunned them momentarily. By the time they had collected their wits only a generous patch of fused sand and a choking concentration of ozone marked the spot where the bolt had struck.

"Bad!" said Nevill. "Worst I've seen. It's striking low ground, which means we have no possible cover out here. Best throw away any metal you may have on you and try to crawl back nearer to the cat—but for Pete's sake keep your heads low."

Another bolt of lightning, bigger and nearer than the first, stabbed into the sand behind them like the bursting of a shell, followed by three almost simultaneously in the near vicinity.

Desperately slowly the party crawled back towards the cat, which stood as the pitifully-low high-spot of this particular area of terrain. On all sides of them now the jagged lightning cut into the ground with burning shafts of vicious energy, like the arrows of retribution fired by some crazed

electric god. Then a shaft burned down on the cat itself.
The fantastic current fused the metal into a white-hot bauble
which was ripped open by the expanding air within. Before
their horrified eyes the cat sank like a lead toy thrown on
to glowing embers, and became a dirty, slag-shot puddle of
mixed metal and silicates alloying with the red sand of Tazoo.

Then mercifully it began to rain. Nevill turned his face
to the stinging, acrid precipitation and let out a howl of
pure relief. A few seconds later they were running like half-
blinded madmen through the corrosive waters in the direction of the base camp, heedless now of the cracking lightning
which had withdrawn to the edge of the rain belt. They
were fortunately within a few steps of the base when the
wall of sharp, abrasive sand, whipped to fury by a fantastic driving wind, bore down upon them out of the deep
purples of the approaching night.

TWO

"Welcome to Tazoo, Lieutenant!" Colonel Nash beckoned
him into the office.

Fritz explored the still-smarting skin on his face and hands,
and was still painfully aware of the puffiness around his
eyes. "Thank you, Colonel. That was quite an initiation
ceremony out there!"

Colonel Nash smiled fleetingly. "Unpremeditated, I assure
you, but the weather is part of the reason you're here. A
ground-cat is the toughest machine available, but as you
saw for yourself it is totally incapable of standing up to the
environment. The low pH of the celestial waters conspires
with the sand to etch and tear the guts out of any transportation contrivance we've yet imported to Tazoo. When you
consider atmospheric chlorine, hydrogen chloride, free sulphuric acid and ozone, plus high humidity and extreme
ultraviolet radiation together with an additional nightly sandblast, you can guess that corrosion prevention is not the
least of our troubles."

Fritz shuddered involuntarily.

"I must admit," said Nash, "that I haven't always seen
eye to eye with you before on the subject of unorthodox
engineering, but if you can solve our transport problem I
shall at least be open to persuasion. Certainly no orthodox

engineers can give us transport on Tazoo at a cost less than the total budget for the entire enterprise."

"What facilities have we?" asked Fritz.

"On Tazoo—anything you can find. If you need anything shipped out from Terra you'll need a damn good case to get it because of shipping costs. Certainly we can't afford to bring any more vehicles out here. Now it's up to you to delve into your unorthodoxy and come up with something practical."

"How is the Tazoon enterprise going?" asked Fritz.

"Slowly," said Nash, "largely because of the aforementioned transport limitations. Nevill's team have uncovered a lot of architectural monstrosities, but the real prize will come if they can find some of the Tazoon mechanical artifacts. If they do, and if they are one half as weird as the rest of the finds so far, it will require all of your peculiar genius to identify and interpret them. We're expecting to find some very unorthodox engineering from a culture which died before the end of the Pliocene period on Terra."

"What signs are there to indicate that they had a highly scientific culture?" asked Fritz. "Surely the finds so far don't indicate very much."

"The preliminary survey party found signs that the Tazoons had reached both of the Tazoon satellites, and we're reasonably certain that they also reached the next planet sunward in this system and actually established a base there."

"All this sounds highly promising," said Fritz. "But two million years is a long time. Would there be anything left of machines and mechanisms after such a period?"

"Nevill theorizes that to develop a high-level functional civilization the Tazoons must have had some pretty good engineers who would have been making due allowance for the make-up of the Tazoon atmosphere. Furthermore, the moist conditions don't penetrate very far down into the sand, so that the deeper an artifact is buried the greater are its chances of almost infinite survival. Deep exploration at a really promising site should give us a slice of Tazoon civilization in a very reasonable state of preservation. We need only one good site to justify the whole Tazoon enterprise."

The next day Fritz found Philip Nevill in the Archaeological H.Q., apparently none the worse for his previous day's exposure.

"Hullo, Fritz, my boy! What can we do for you?"

"I hope you can answer a question. Do you know what happened to the Tazoons themselves—I mean, why did they become extinct so swiftly when they had achieved such an apparently high technological level?"

Nevill scowled. "You're equating technology with the ability to manipulate environment and thus ensure a higher survival potential. Well, I'm afraid I can't answer that. Indications are that they abandoned the populated areas *en-masse* and migrated towards the equatorial regions. From distribution figures it looks as though the entire population set out for the tropics and were decimated on the way. This suggests they were fleeing from something biologically intolerable which claimed a great number in flight."

"Drastic climatic change?" asked Fritz.

"Climatic, no—environmental, possibly. We looked for evidence of major climatic changes, but there's nothing significant that we can trace. The only thing that is recent, geologically speaking, is the sand."

"The sand?"

"Mm! Probably the result of some ecological imbalance. The major plains appear to have once included prolific forests such as are still to be found in places around the temperate belts. For some reason, drought or fire or blight perhaps, these forests died. The results were typically Terran in their pattern."

"Soil erosion?"

"Yes, and on a catastrophic scale. Once the sand got to work on the unprotected soil nothing thereafter got the chance to germinate. We're still picking up viable seeds from the deep diggings, but all the shallow seeds are either dead or had started growth and been uprooted."

"When did this happen—the erosion?"

"We can't tell with certainty, but it appears to slightly pre-date the extinction of the Tazoons themselves. Whether these two factors are related is something only further research can prove. Does that answer your question?"

"Yes, but only to pose another," said Fritz. "I don't understand how any culture technically able to explore the neighbouring satellites could have been wiped out by anything as foreseeable and reversible as soil erosion. And why migrate to the tropics when the soil fertility remained in the temperate belts?"

"I don't know," said Nevill. "It's a difficult problem. The Tazoons were not even humanoid, and the probability is that neither their physiology nor their logic had anything in common with our own. It could be misleading if we attempted to interpret their actions by simple extrapolation of what we might have done in similar circumstances."

"A good point," said Fritz. "I don't necessarily agree with it, but I'll bear it in mind. Thanks, Philip, you've given me something to think about."

Having established that the U.E. squad was reasonably well quartered, Fritz turned his attention to the transport problem. This brought him back to Jacko who had compiled a transport survey which he presented with as much enthusiasm as if it had been his own death warrant.

"We're in trouble, Fritz. Of the hundred ground-cats originally provided for the enterprise only twenty are still functioning. Two hundred hours operating life on Tazoo reduces a cat to a condition where you couldn't sell it for scrap value. By sorting bits and pieces we could probably reconstruct another five cats, but we can only reckon on a maximum of six thousand operating-cat-hours before we start walking."

Fritz stared disconsolately at a virgin notebook. "What about tractors and heavy equipment?"

"They're not too bad—but only by virtue of the fact that most of them are still in sealed crates. Once they're broken-out there's no reason to suppose they'll last any longer than the cats do. This combination of corrosion and abrasion is something to which I'd not cheerfully expose a clockwork mouse."

"I take your point," said Fritz. "As I see the present requirements it doesn't give us much over a sixty-day transport potential. What protection can we give to the cats to extend their working life?"

"A lot of a vehicle we can plastic coat, as they do with the Knudsens. The engines are a more difficult problem. Some genius thought of providing them with standard aluminium-alloy turbine housings, and what the Tazoon atmosphere does to the alloy makes my flesh creep. Even the vitreous liners devitrify and release particles of silica into the bearings."

"Don't bother to describe," said Fritz, "what silica does

to the bearings. I think we have to face the fact that while we might save most of the cats themselves we aren't going to be able to save many of the engines. We could devise a system of enclosing the engines in an inert atmosphere— but I doubt if we have the facilities here to do a permanent job. We then also need a supply of controlled pH, moisture-free oxygen for the air intake. I think we could produce that by electrolysis, but I doubt if we can handle it in sufficient quantities to be of much value."

"And so on *ad-infinitum*," said Jacko ruefully.

Fritz nodded. "Let's try it anyway. I want two cats modified. Plastic spray them everywhere possible, and seal the engine compartment and fill it with a nitrogen and hydrogen mixture of non-ignitable composition. Get our micro-Linde column working for the nitrogen and make an electrolysis plant for the hydrogen. You'll need both the Linde and the electrolytic plant to get enough oxygen for the air-supply for the engine intakes, and you'd better dilute the oxygen with any nitrogen you can spare, then adjust the turbines to run on that."

"And what do I keep the oxygen in?" asked Jacko.

"They've a fair supply of the plastic poly-polymer they use for spraying the huts. It shouldn't be beyond our capacity to blow a gasbag from that."

"It all sounds feasible," said Jacko, "but I doubt the capacity of the micro-Linde to give us all the nitrogen we need."

"So do I," said Fritz, "that's why I said to modify two cats only. There's plenty of other things to try, but this is the most obvious, and we've neither time nor the resources to start nitrogen fixation in a big way." He went to the window, opened the shutter and stared moodily out at the red and featureless wasteland.

"Sand," he said. "Nothing but sand, fine-grained, abrasive and all-pervading. What we need, Jacko, is something completely new in the way of transport on Tazoo. I wonder what the Tazoons themselves employed."

Three days later and the modification of the cats was in full swing when the telephone rang.

"Van Noon speaking."

"Fritz, Nevill here. I've got some work for you."

"Bring it over," said Fritz. "A little more won't make much difference."

"Right. Be with you in about ten minutes. It's one of these Tazoon mechanisms we've been looking for."

"Now you have me interested," said Fritz. "Exactly what is it?"

"That's what I want you to tell me."

Ten minutes later Nevill arrived and ceremonially knocked out his pipe on the threshold in deference to a large no-smoking notice over the jury-rigged electrolysis plant. Then he signalled to his assistants who dragged a large object into the hut and dropped it on the floor. Fritz looked at it dubiously.

"I think you've come to the wrong department. It looks like the great grandaddy of an alien chicken wishbone once belonging to some grandaddy alien chicken. Why not present it to the biology boys?"

"I did," said Nevill, "but they sent it right back with the message that you were responsible for investigating machinery."

"Machinery?" Fritz surveyed the acquisition moodily. "Have you tried it on the catering department? Perhaps they could turn it into some sort of broth."

"Machinery," said Nevill firmly. "And I'll tell you why. It isn't animal, it's vegetable—Tazoon ironwood to be precise. Also, it didn't grow that way. It was manufactured, or at least trimmed to shape, as witness the tooling marks. Furthermore, the Tazoons were plenty fond of them because the Southern plain out yonder has them at an estimated density of nearly half a million to the square kilometre."

Fritz choked for a full half minute. "Half a million?"

Nevill nodded. "And that plain is pretty big. If the sampling we have done is representative of the whole area there could be something like five thousand million of those on that one plain alone. I know the Tazoons were alien beyond our conception of the word, but I just can't see them producing that many just for the hell of it. That would be an exercise akin to paving the Sahara desert with pencil sharpeners. It's my belief that the wishbones are something functional. I want you to tell me what they were and what their function was."

Fritz nodded. "I'll let you have a preliminary report in a day or so, but if that's a machine I should hate to see their idea of a great big alien chicken wishbone."

After Nevill had left, Fritz spent a quiet hour examining the wishbone from all angles and going all over the surface of it with a magnifying glass looking for clues as to its function. Then Jacko had the wishbone hauled to the workshop for a more thorough examination. He reported back when the work was completed.

"I think we have something here, Fritz. You know those nodules on the inner surfaces, well, the fluoroscope shows a dark mass of some foreign material in each. If you're agreeable we're proposing to cut one out and see what it is."

"Start cutting," Fritz said, "because if this is a sample of Tazoon engineering then the sooner we start to come to grips with it the better."

Reluctantly the bandsaw cut into the ancient ironwood. Halfway through, the blade screeched complainingly on some hard inclusion. Then the nodule became detached, and from inside it Jacko shook a large, bright crystal on to the table.

"I thought as much," said Fritz. "There are metal fibres in the structure of the wishbone and metallized facets on the crystal. On this evidence I'd say this was some form of piezo-electric device. And see how the crystal is drilled— do you suppose there could have been strings across the wishbone?"

Jacko counted the nodules equal on both sides. "Lord, a harp!" he said in a voice heavy with incredulity.

"Or a sound-transducer," said Fritz. "There are common electrical paths through the ironwood, and connections to the crystals. If you applied an alternating current to those contacts, the crystals would excite the strings in sympathy according to the resonant frequency of the particular system. I wonder what on earth it would sound like? Jacko, start re-stringing what's left of this thing while I sort out a power amplifier and a few bits and pieces. Together we can make some be-eautiful music."

"Right," said Jacko, "but if your conception of music is anything like your engineering I'm going to take time out to make some earplugs too."

THREE

It took three hours to complete the assembly. Fritz disappeared to the communications hut and returned with an assortment of equipment which he appeared to assemble more by inspiration than by design. When everything was ready he switched on. The first results were shattering, and the electronics needed drastic revision before a reasonably tolerable result was obtained.

After some final adjustments Fritz pronounced himself satisfied with the results and dropped into a chair to listen attentively, his gaze wandering to the open shutter and the blood-red sunset trailing nakedly beyond.

"Listen to it, Jacko!" said Fritz happily. "Alien and beautiful beyond recall."

"I might just point out," said Jacko, "that if somebody attempted to re-string a two-million years old grand piano with stranded cable and without any idea of the scale and pitch involved, the results would sound equally alien."

"I'm in no mood to quibble with one who possesses such a tiny soul," said Fritz. "To me this is music such as the ancient Tazoons knew it as they walked hand in hand in the eyeless evenings of old Tazoo. Can't you imagine it, Jacko, this incredible music voiced by a million harps in the blood-red twilight of this alien land?"

"It makes my head ache," said Jacko. "What are you feeding into the blasted thing, anyway?"

Fritz coughed. "Actually it's the telemetry signals from the satellite monitoring the Tazoon ionosphere, but the harp contributes about five-hundred per cent distortion, so you never know it from music."

"I can't help feeling distinctly uneasy," said Jacko, "about the notion of anybody wanting half a million crazy self-playing harps to the square kilometre. No culture could be that fond of music and yet survive."

"They didn't survive. And we can't yet hope to understand so alien a culture. If you want a parallel, think of all the millions of personal transistor radios taken to the beaches on Terra on a public holiday. Think how much simpler life would be if they erected loudspeakers at four-foot intervals on all beaches and made full-time listening compulsory instead of merely unavoidable."

Despite the warmth Jacko shuddered visibly and closed his eyes, while the complex tones of the harp sang strangely with unfathomable harmonies which did curious things to his stomach. "I'm beginning to get the idea," he said, "exactly why the Tazoons decided to migrate. Listening to this, I get precisely the same urge myself."

At that moment the door was flung open and Nevill, eyes aglow with jubilation, burst into the hut.

"Fritz, we've done it! A real find at last. To judge from

the extent of our soundings we seem to have hit upon the location of a whole damn Tazoon city under the sand."

Fritz bounded up with enthusiasm. "Congratulations, Philip! This sounds like the breakthrough we've been waiting for. Exactly where is this site?"

"Under our very noses—about twenty kilometres east of here. I tell you, Fritz, my boy, there's a real metropolis down there."

He stopped, aware for the first time of the singing harp. "What in the name of Thunder is that?"

"A genuine Tazoon harp in action," said Fritz modestly. "Don't you like it?"

"No," said Nevill, "because it isn't right. Nobody, however alien, would want more than one of anything that sounds like that. Besides"—he mopped the moisture which had risen on his brow—"the Tazoons had very small ear cavities. Their audible range was undoubtedly in the medium ultrasonic. Frankly they could never have heard anything pitched as low as that. Sorry! Try and make it do something else like lighting fires or something."

And so saying, he was gone, leaving Fritz looking miserably at his equipment and trying to avoid Jacko's eyes.

"All right," said Fritz, "so even I can't always be right first time." He turned off the amplifier disconsolately. "I still think it was a good idea."

"That's the second of your good ideas that has run off the rails today," said Jacko, fingering his ears.

"Second?" Fritz looked mildly surprised.

"Yes, I forgot to tell you. Your idea for obtaining pure nitrogen for the cats by fractional distillation in the micro-Linde didn't solve the problem, it merely transferred it. The blasted Tazoon atmosphere's eaten the guts out of the Linde compressor."

"That was all I needed to make my day!" said Fritz. "You'd better get the boys together, Jacko. I want every repairable ground-cat and tractor prepared for operation, and as much heavy lifting and moving tackle as we can acquire."

"What are you planning, Fritz?"

"Let's face it, Jacko, we can't keep enough transport in service to do the daily forty-kilometre round-trips to the new site for very long. If that's a major site they've found there won't be much point in having a base camp this far distant. The logical thing to do is expend all our resources, moving the whole base to the new site."

"Are you crazy?" asked Jacko. "It'd take months to dismantle this lot and transport it that far."

"I said nothing about dismantling. A Knudsen hut is a unit structure. It is capable of being moved as a whole. Can you think of any reason why we shouldn't just attach a cat or tractor to each hut and haul it bodily over the sand to the new site?"

"Yes, Colonel Nash and the base psychiatrist, to name only two. A Knudsen could never stand a belting like that and finish in one piece."

"Ordinarily, no, but these have been covered with alternate layers of resin and sand to a thickness which has become ridiculous. Dammit, Jacko, you've got a metal and sand-filled resin laminate there which must have all of a hundred and fifty times the strength of the original hut."

"You're dead right, of course," said Jacko. "But I'm going to love thinking of you trying to explain it to Colonel Nash."

"All right," said Nash at last. "You can start moving the base just as soon as the necessary cables and services have been laid. I don't need to remind you that everything has to be fully secured by sundown. And I warn you that if anything goes wrong . . ."

He leaned back speculatively for a moment.

"You know, Fritz, I must confess I'm disappointed. I'd expected great things from unorthodoxy, but when it comes to the point you can't even promise to keep a decent transport system in operation."

"A snowflake," Fritz protested, "wouldn't stand much chance in Hell unless you had a ton of refrigeration equipment alongside. The fault is not being in Hell, but in being a snowflake. You've got a roughly similar position with your cats on Tazoo. A suitable cat could easily be designed for these conditions, but it would need Terran resources to build it and a long haul to bring it out here. The cost would be astronomical. The limitation is in associating transport with the idea of a ground-cat."

"I'm perfectly aware of that," said Nash. "In fact it's the reason I sent for you. You have the reputation for producing the impossible at very short notice. All right—I challenge you to produce."

"Miracles we perform immediately," said Fritz quietly. "The impossible takes a little longer. After all, we've only been here a week."

Nash watched him narrowly for a moment. "Fritz, frankly I don't believe anybody has the remotest chance of doing what I ask, but I'm calling your bluff. If you have any sort of transport running on Tazoo in three months' time I'll be glad to take back all the harsh things I've ever said about U.E. If you don't I'll have to send you back to Terra. The Tazoon enterprise wasn't designed to carry any dead weight."

"It's a challenge I'll accept," said Fritz, "but don't expect to equate transportation with any vehicular form you're used to, because the chances are a million to one against it looking like anything you've ever seen before."

Jacko was waiting for him outside the office.

"Bad?" he asked.

"Not good," said Fritz. "We've got three months to crack the transport problem or get kicked out as a bunch of no-good layabouts. The honour—even the continuance of U.E. —is very much at stake. Somehow we've got to contrive some sort of vehicle, and this in the face of the fact that we have no source of constructional material capable of withstanding the Tazoon environment."

"So where do we go from here, Fritz?"

"Damned if I know. You go and check the arrangements for the big move. I'm going over to the site to see how friend Nevill is doing. He may have dug up a little inspiration out there—and Heaven knows I could use a little right now."

Nevill saw the cat drawing across the rouge desert, and came to the edge of the workings to await Fritz's arrival.

"How're things going, Philip?"

"Wonderful, my boy. We knew we had a major find, but this—this is paradise! We're going straight down on a major city by the look of it, and the stuff on the lower levels where the sand is dry is in a perfect state of preservation. Some of the three-storied buildings are so sound that we'll be able to use them for our own purposes. I tell you, Fritz, the Tazoon enterprise looks like paying off about two million per cent interest. The complete analysis of the stuff found here will occupy generations."

Fritz gazed down into the broad quarry which was the site of the workings. On every hand the feverish activity of the archaeological teams pointed a measure of the excitement and enthusiasm which infected everyone concerned. The shifts had been voluntarily lengthened, but even so, the end of the shirt period had to be declared a compulsory cessation of work lest those on the trail of such immeasurable archaeological delights should endanger their health by continuing until they dropped from exhaustion.

Here and there alien towers were already exposed above the sand, unimaginable obelisks of incomprehensible architecture, curiously distorted and decayed by time and the ravages of wind and sand. Some, the sand shored back to greater depths, were firmer on the lower levels, and the architecture was even more marvellously and more inconceivably wrought. Occasionally, vertical pits descended at points where logic had decreed there lay something more intriguing or exciting or yielding greater bounty for the effort it entailed.

Fritz was fascinated beyond measure. The clawing otherworldliness drew his imagination on with an inescapable lure. As an engineer he fought to tame the logic of the structures which were being uncovered before him, but something in his soul, poesy perhaps, denied him an identification of parts and trapped him in the wonder of the whole. He was the technologist who came for a dispassionate analysis and stayed to worship.

With great resolve he wrenched his mind from its journeyings and looked at Nevill appealingly. The latter patted him on the shoulder sympathetically. "I know, my boy," he said. "It takes us all like that. It's both wonderful and sad to be uncovering the remains of so great a culture: wonderful because the culture was so great, and sad because we find their city empty of the creatures who created it."

"Why the hell did they have to go?" asked Fritz. "After they'd got all this way? They had mastered their environment to a degree comparable to ourselves, then in the space of a few short centuries they faded and died away and the sand moved in and covered all their marvels. But for what reason did they go? It's something we must discover lest it also comes upon us."

FOUR

By sundown the last hut had been transferred to its new position near the workings. The day had been one of great activity intermixed with frustration. As Fritz had foreseen the huts had proved themselves capable of being moved bodily across the sand, but the condition of the cats and tractors was such that the path of the move was plainly marked with a trail of abandoned vehicles spread broadly across the sandy steppes. Indeed, by the end of the day only five cats remained in operation.

After organizing a team to recover any repairable cats, Jacko went to look for Fritz and found him in the workshop idly strumming the Tazoon harp with the air of a man evoking the muses as an aid to inspiration.

"You know, Jacko, I wish I could work out what happened to the Tazoons. I simply can't understand why such a highly advanced and organized culture should suddenly fall to pieces. There's no suggestion of a major war, and there's not sufficient radioactive material on the planet to make a nuclear holocaust a possibility. It's a highly disturbing thought that a catastrophe which could destroy a race with that level of technology could leave so little trace. It's as though they suddenly closed up their cities and walked out to die on a mass trek to the equator."

"What about famine?" asked Jacko.

"Possibly. That's virtually what Nevill suggested—widespread soil erosion. For some reason the major forests in this zone died suddenly. That rather suggests a prolonged drought—but you'd think a major technology fighting for survival could cope with even that. The sea is an atrocious mineral stew, but I'm willing to bet you could distil enough water to maintain a pretty fair agricultural belt if the need arose."

"But without nuclear energy where would you get that sort of power?" asked Jacko. "Distillation of sea-water on that scale would take a great deal of energy."

"Power!" Fritz sat up. "Now there's an idea! Come to think of it, where did they get their power from anyway? Let's put a few facts together. We know that at a certain stage in the history of Tazoo something happened—something which in the span of a couple of centuries destroyed the civilized inhabitants of the planet. Curiously, the wild-life forms survived for a considerable time afterwards, and some are still to be found in the forest belts. Now the basic difference between civilized and wild-life forms is that the former are power dependent animals while the latter are not. Jacko, my dear fellow, you may have hit upon something there."

"It's just a gift," said Jacko modestly.

"Then seeing it didn't cost you anything, see if you can stretch it a little further. Let's play for a moment with the assumption that the Tazoons had become power-dependent animals—as we have ourselves. What would their basic source of energy have been if it could have failed suddenly and disastrously?"

"Oil or natural gas, perhaps," said Jacko.

"Not very convincing. By all appearances the Tazoons were great power users. From what Nevill's uncovered recently I'd say the power consumption in this area alone must have been quite fantastic even by Terran standards. Now, you don't develop a heavy power-consuming technology unless you've a good idea that you have the resources to maintain it. To do otherwise would be technological suicide."

"That's assuming they thought about the problem in the same way that a human being would."

"I wouldn't know about human beings," said Fritz drily, "but engineers I do know about, and their thought processes must be essentially similar whether they have one head or six. There are an infinite number of ways of solving any engineering problem, but the simpler answers will always look familiar. It's just the nature of the beast. Give a ten-armed Dingbat a head of steam and tell him to convert it into electrical energy. I don't care what the influence of his racial characteristics, training or personal geometry, some-where, at some point, he's going to fall into a chain of logic familiar to engineers of similar calibre anywhere. Ergo, I don't think we can go far wrong if we tackle this problem from our own standpoint, and currently we are assuming they had a power supply which appeared infallible yet failed. Now we need to know what was the source of that energy. If we knew that maybe we could work out why it stopped."

The telephone rang and Fritz answered it. Nevill had been searching for him.

"Fritz, I'd like to see you first thing in the morning. There's something I want you to take a look at."

"Right! Something promising?"

"I imagine so. The team has just uncovered something which looks like the entrance to a mine of some sort. Per-haps you'd like to look it over."

"We'll be there first thing," said Fritz.

"What's up?" asked Jacko.

"Nevill's team have discovered what he thinks may be the entrance to a mine."

"In the centre of a city?"

"The same question occurred to me," said Fritz. "I don't think that a mine is particularly probable; though it might just be connected with our lost energy source—or he may have stumbled on something I've been looking for myself."

"What's that?"

"Jacko, in a city as large and as complex as this one appears to be, where's the logical place to put the bulk passenger transport system?"

"Underground," said Jacko, "same as always."

"Precisely, and that's what I'm hoping Nevill's hit upon."

"God!" said Jacko. "An alien subway scarcely bears thinking about."

Further in from the door they had to use flashlights. Here the sand had not penetrated so deeply, and by the time they had reached the head of the shaft only a brief dusting covered the floor.

The shaft was equipped with the normal Tazoon-type stairway—a central pole with round horizontal bars set in a helix, but on a broader pattern than they had encountered hitherto and with a deeper pitch. Such a stairway was not adapted to human physiology, but it was traversable—just—by those with climbing experience or suicidal tendencies. Jacko had neither.

"Down?" he enquired, his flashlight failing to probe the darkness of the alien depths.

"Down," said Fritz. "Where's your sense of adventure?"

"It remained firmly embedded in my childhood," said Jacko, "along with the sense necessary not to get into situations like this."

"Down!" said Fritz firmly, and suited actions to his words.

Together they climbed down perhaps one hundred metres. Since it was impossible both to climb and hold a flashlight, this was accomplished in total darkness, and the steady rhythm of the climb from bar to bar exercised its own almost hypnotic fascination. Both had to stand for many seconds at the bottom to re-orientate their senses.

The preservation of the passageways at that level was remarkable and probably complete, and the air was cooler and less aggressive than above. Remarkable also was the dryness of the connecting tunnels which had lain for so long at such a depth, indicating the complete lack of a water table above the level of the deep-welled seas of Tazoo. The walls here were of metal, curiously wrought in a manner which might have been functional or might have been symbolic; and the alien strangeness of a completely artificial Tazoon environment gripped at their hearts with a half fear which had nothing to do with self-preservation. For the first time they felt the full impact of standing in the presence of the logical but inimaginable achievements of a culture which had no common roots with their own. They could vaguely comprehend but never predict the unfolding of the unearthly technology which surrounded them.

Machine or effigies, they had no means of knowing which, stood like dark, mute sentries in the uncertain, shifting shadows of the flashlamp's beam: the tortuous walls and fluted ceilings were channelled and moulded with a thousand metal mouths connected to unguessable throats for unfathomable reasons—only the floor approximated its Terran counterpart, having a common engineering function of providing an unimpeded pedestrian passageway.

They turned another corner and stopped abruptly when the flashlamps' beams soared into empty darkness and encountered nothing. Their consternation was relieved by the realization that they were now looking along the length of a vastly greater tunnel than any they had so far traversed. Vaguely they could trace the complex vaulted roof rising to its apex in a series of panels shaped to some intriguing algebraic equation. At their feet the floor continued unchanged as far as the flash-beams could reveal, while to their right the level dropped abruptly perhaps two metres to form a channel of about seven metres width. Beyond the channel rose the walls again arching upwards.

"Are you thinking what I'm thinking?" asked Fritz.

"Uh!" said Jacko. "No matter how you build it, a subway station is a subway station, and this is just one such."

"Good man," said Fritz. "I want to have a look at the rails."

Together they surveyed the channel, probing minutely with their flashlights.

"No lines," said Jacko at last, his voice tinged with disappointment. "It could be that we're wrong about this place. Perhaps a sewer . . ."

"I'm not wrong," said Fritz. "I'd know a subway when I

found one even if I was deaf, blind and shut up in a box.
It's part of the chemistry of whatever genes conspire to make
an engineer. Here, help me down, I want to explore."

"Don't you think we'd better go back and get some re-
inforcements?" said Jacko. Fritz had started along the channel to where it entered a somewhat smaller tunnel undeni-
ably reminiscent of a Terran subway. "For Heaven's sake,
Fritz, you don't know what you might find in there!"

"What's eating you, Jacko? Not losing your nerve all of
a sudden?"

"No, it's just that walking down a tunnel that *might* contain an emergent subway train goes against my finer sensi-
bilities—even if it is two million years behind schedule."

Fritz took fifteen paces into the tunnel and let out a whoop
which paralysed Jacko with fright.

"Jacko, get down here quick! I've found one."

"Found one what?" asked Jacko when he had regained
control of his vocal cords.

"A train, you idiot. I've found a blessed train! Fetch the
other lamp."

Against his better judgment Jacko dropped into the channel
and followed Fritz into the tunnel. Then with a churning
stomach and racing brain he examined the artifact which
barred their further entry.

"That," he asked finally, "is a train?"

"It can't be anything else," said Fritz, not very happily.
"It doesn't appear to be a signal box and there's not much
point in having a wrought-iron summer house this far underground. It appears to be the right shape to fit the tunnel
so it's probably either a highly ornate tunnelling machine or
else it's a train."

"Alien!" said Jacko in awe. "The connotations of that
word get lost by common usage. It doesn't begin to convey
the mind-twisting sense that everything you know and believe
has been scrunched up and re-sorted by a different kind of
logic. These people had different values and different basics,
and it makes the mind squirm even trying to re-adjust."

"They didn't have different basics," said Fritz, "they merely
had a different emphasis on the relative values of the same
old basics. We can't yet try to comprehend the culture, but
when it comes to unravelling their engineering I think we
shall find we have a great deal in common."

"Like an iron-lace potting-shed without wheels or tracks

which we presume to be a train simply because it doesn't appear to be anything else?"

"Just so," said Fritz. "We have to separate the mechanics from the culture. As far as we've gone we've found very few Tazoon applications of principles of which we were completely ignorant. Of course, they were streets ahead of us in some fields and curiously lacking in others—they had no organic chemistry, for instance. But they don't appear to have dabbled in the occult, so if that's a train it's only a matter of time before we find out what made it go."

Cautiously they squeezed down between the curious vehicle and the tunnel wall, the better to examine the structure's complexity and strangeness.

"It's a crazy, twisted birdcage," said Jacko finally. "An appliance for containing crazy, twisted birds."

Fritz looked up from the complex of curiously wrought mechanisms. "We'd better get some more lights down here, and muster some of the squad. I want this insane dumpling-container taken to pieces and put together again when I've had a chance to examine the pieces."

"Cannibalization I can understand," said Jacko, "but why the resurrection?"

"Because," said Fritz Van Noon, "if it's the last thing I do I'm going to put the subways of Tazoo back in operation. We obviously can't build a transportation system on the surface, but here we have a ready-made nucleus which already goes halfway to meet the problem."

"I demand to be invalided out of the Service on the grounds of insanity," said Jacko, "your insanity. I thought we'd had enough of railways up on Cannis."

"That was different," said Fritz. "There we were merely up against physical obstacles such as errant volcanoes. This is specifically an exercise in matching technologies. All we have to do is to determine which part of the railway system moves and which part is intended to stay still. That shouldn't be too difficult, now should it?"

"Not when reduced to such basic terms," Jacko agreed dourly. "But I know you. You never realize when you're beaten."

"I've told you before," said Fritz sternly, "there's no such thing as a physical impossibility. A limitation is a state of mind, not a question of fact. Here we are faced with the work of a completely alien race who nevertheless had a technological and scientific level roughly comparable to our own. Providing we hold that one fact paramount we ought to be able to unscramble any device this planet has to offer—and make it function for our own service if we wish."

"Providing one thing holds good," said Jacko. "We have first to be able to recognize a thing for what it is. It's no good dismantling a Tazoon milk-strainer if we're under the impression that it ought to be a transistor superhet—or *vice-versa,* come to think of it."

FIVE

Fritz reported back to Philip Nevill. The latter listened to the details of the find with the air of suppressed jubilation which was rapidly becoming his permanent expression. Then he ran his fingers through his untidy hair and searched for his pipe with a distracted grin.

"Fritz, my boy, this is perfectly marvellous. What a day we've had! We've opened up so many promising new lines of research that the whole damned thing is getting out of hand. We could do with five hundred trained archaeologists to digest the meat in this lot, and even then we couldn't do more than scratch the surface. The impact of building techniques alone on Terra is going to be fantastic, and when the whole complex is assembled into Terran know-how its impact on the human race will be so great that our own culture will never be quite the same again.

"If you really want to make your mark on the enterprise, then take over this subway completely, because I shan't be able to get round to it for five years at least. Do a complete technical run-down on it, as detailed as you like. Do anything you like with it which won't impair its archaeological value. All I ask is a comprehensive progress report in time for each data shipment to Terra."

"Fair enough!" said Fritz. "I want to open up the buildings directly above the station to look for ancillaries."

Nevill glanced at his sketch map and drew a line through two diagrammatical blocks. "It's all yours," he said, "but don't drive yourself daft trying to comprehend too much too fast. You'll find you have to absorb Tazoon environments rather than understand them. Sooner or later the pieces fit themselves into place. And Heaven knows there's enough pieces available for fitting—a jigsaw embracing the life and work of a complete culture."

"We've just got ourselves a subway," said Fritz, as he re-joined Jacko at the workings. "We're going to open up the building here and see what's inside."

"Who's we?" asked Jacko suspiciously.

"You," said Fritz. "I'm going below again to see if I can trace any control sequence running up from below. I want you to go in there and see if you can find anything similar running down. We'll meet at the end of the shift and com-pare notes. You know what to look for—cable groupings or anything which suggests that it might have a control or power function."

"You're really set on this, aren't you?" Jacko said. "About using it, I mean."

"Certainly," said Fritz. "Let's face it, if Fritz Van Noon can't restart an alien subway then who in the universe would you expect to be able to do it?"

"I was afraid you'd ask that," said Jacko.

An hour later they met again at the portals of the building.

"There's a sort of power and control complex which ap-pears to come down somewhere near the further end here," said Fritz.

Jacko nodded. "I picked up the end of that," he said. "There's a channel running through the basement of the building, and the complex rises into that, and is then split into sections which are fed to the floors above."

"What's it like in there?" asked Fritz.

"Weird," said Jacko. "There's no other word to describe it. It's like the epitaph to an insane, overgrown spider with a compulsive spite against inverted single-head broaching presses."

"Thank you," said Fritz. "I can imagine it all too clearly."

Jacko's description of the basement of the building was, if anything, an understatement. The ground floor proved in-conceivably worse, and the situation deteriorated rapidly as they ascended to the higher floors. The subway had pos-sessed the crude simplicity of a functional unit, but the de-tail and complexity of the levels in the building above defied analysis or description. For a long time no object which they examined provided any sort of clue as to its function, and they traversed the cluttered levels with an increasing sense of dismay and frustration. As with most of the larger build-ings only the top storeys had suffered any considerable de-cay, and the sand and damp had not penetrated into the interiors to any great extent, so that the state of preservation on the levels in which they were interested was excellent.

Fritz's spirits were nearing their lowest ebb as he battled with an ocean of incomprehensibilities, until he entered the final gallery. Here he stopped, groping for form in the alien pattern, then seized a glimpse of illuminated understanding and fanned it into a flame.

"Jacko! Do you know what this is? Don't you see—electrical control gear."

Jacko was unimpressed. "If this is their idea of electrical control gear I should hate to see their version of a collection of crazy, twisted maypoles."

"It doesn't matter," said Fritz. "The approach may be alien, but the underlying logic is inescapable. Unless I miss my guess this is an automatic switching system, and from its complexity I should think it's pretty comprehensive. It may even be the only switching system for the whole of the Tazoon subways. You realize what that means?"

"About fifteen years' circuit analysis," said Jacko morosely.

"No. Look at the condition of this stuff. The preservation is as good here as it is in the subway itself. The chances are it's still functional. We'd only have to re-connect the power to get the whole thing back into operation."

"Perish the thought!" said Jacko. "I may be a bit naïve, but assuming—just for the sake of argument—that what we've found is a subway, where would you get the energy to power it? Subways need a lot of power, and if the Tazoons ran out of it how are you going to find it?"

"We'll worry about that later. It may not be easy, but I have one advantage the Tazoons didn't have—access to the complete technologies and resources of a scientific culture which was completely alien to the Tazoons. I don't doubt that Colonel Nash could be persuaded to bring an MHD oscillating-plasma generator out from Terra, but that's a last resort. As an unorthodox engineer I'd prefer to locate the original Tazoon power source and see if a completely fresh engineering approach could start it producing again."

"So what's the plan?" asked Jacko.

"Get Harris and a couple of the electrical boys to join me here to try and analyse the circuit logic. Meanwhile you take the rest of the squad below and start dismantling the train. Between us we should discover enough about the way the Tazoons handled electricity and mechanisms to have a fair idea of how to make these pieces work."

"You think so?" asked Jacko. "I still haven't forgotten what you did to that ruddy harp."

Fritz's team did indeed manage to establish a certain amount of circuit logic, and once a few principles were known the work progressed rapidly. They concentrated mainly on the huge switching columns, swiftly realizing that what at first sight could be mistaken for relative crudity was in fact an ingenious and sophisticated short-cut technique to solve a highly complex sequence-switching problem. Among other things they discovered that the assembly was probably built to handle alternating current with an efficiency peaking at about ten kilocycles a second, although such periodicity seemed unlikely in practice. The current handling capacity of the assembly was staggeringly high. Breakdown voltages too were high, but afforded no real clues as to the normal operating potentials. Safety precautions against unshielded conductors were non-existent, and they were forced to the conclusion that either the equipment was designed to operate unattended or else the physiology of the Tazoons had rendered them immune to electric shocks which would be lethal to their Terran counterparts. The apparatus which logically should have been metering equipment, however, made no sense at all.

Somebody was soon at work rigging up a communicator to connect the switching gallery with the subway below. When the line was functional Jacko was the first to make a call.

"Fritz, we've run into a snag on this train dismantling project. We can't get the blasted thing apart. Tell me I'm crazy if you like, but I'd swear the train was cast as a whole and not fabricated—moving parts included."

"Cast in a pattern of that complexity in steel?" asked Fritz incredulously.

"Not steel," said Jacko. "Titanium, unless I judge my metals wrong."

"That only makes it worse," said Fritz. "Come to think of it, we were being a bit naïve expecting a two-million-year extinct culture to leave something which could be dismantled with a hammer and a pair of Stillsons. Is there no hope at all?"

"We could take an atomic-hydrogen torch or a cutting laser and chop it into two-inch slices, but I doubt if Nevill would react favourably to the idea."

"Come to think of it," said Fritz, "neither would I. Better abandon the project, Jacko, and come back up here. I think I've got a better idea anyway."

"What are you planning now, Fritz?"

"I'm looking at it this way: there are two ways of making a piece of equipment yield the secret of its function—you can dismantle it and worry the principle out of its components, or you can simply set it operating."

"I hope I'm misunderstanding you," said Jacko. "For one ghastly moment I had the idea you were proposing to re-start the Tazoon subway without knowing how it worked."

"I was proposing just that. Can you think of a faster way of finding out how it works than by seeing it in action?"

"Is one allowed to resign from the project?" asked Jacko. "Or is suicide the only logical form of escape?"

"You can also be beaten to death by your superior officer, if you're really smitten with an escapist death-wish. We think we've unscrambled the power lines in the gallery here and we've made a guess at what should prove to be the main input lines."

"So?"

"So I want to trace them back to source. Then we can start investigating whether or not we can re-start the native power producing plant. I want every man I can get employed on tracing those lines, Jacko, and I want you to supervise personally. Remember, we have to get the whole thing operational inside three months if we're to beat Nash's deadline."

"I still think it's a waste of time," said Jacko. "If we're right that the Tazoon civilization collapsed because of lack of power, what chance have we of finding it some two million years later?"

"I suspect the answer is quantitative," said Fritz. "They were trying to run a civilization, we're trying only to run a subway. I'd estimate our requirements at perhaps one ten-millionth of theirs or less. Viewed in that light it doesn't seem too difficult a task, now does it?"

SIX

Nevill's team had concentrated on clearing only the tops of the taller buildings. Generally the sand penetration into the interiors was not total, and thus they had access to large modules of Tazoon architectural environment without having to wait for the total clearance which ultimately would follow as resources became available. Once gaining the interior of a building they were relatively free to explore the entire contents of the lower levels. Archaeologically the finds were so incredibly lush that complete classification and analysis would take many decades, and the method therefore used was to set up specialist study groups to make a complete analysis of certain typical areas as a guide to rapidly separating the unique from the mundane when new areas were opened up. Representative samples were carefully crated for transport to Terra, where a more exhaustive examination would be undertaken.

For the next two weeks Fritz himself was kept fully employed in his role as authority on alien science and technology, and the sheer mass of work confronting him could have kept him comfortably occupied for several lifetimes at least. It was now painfully obvious that the staff of the Tazoon enterprise could have been increased a hundredfold and still the finds would have been more numerous than the researchers. Fritz's own work in the field was hampered by the fact that he was working without assistance, the entire complement of the U.E. squad being devoted to locating the elusive power source from which the Tazoons had derived their supply.

On this latter point even Nevill had been unable to offer any help. Although detailed maps of the sectors of the buried city were beginning to be built up there was nothing in them which suggested any power generation or distribution facilities. This was not conclusive, because in very few areas had it yet been possible to excavate below the level of the basic terrain on which the city had been built, and what lay underneath was still a subject for conjecture, but the pattern of conductors disappearing into the depths was sufficient to convince Fritz that whatever the source it was probably not located within the city confines. Jacko's report did not appear to illuminate the situation.

"I tell you, Fritz, that main power input cable you gave us was nothing of the sort. For fifteen blasted days we've traced that thing. A cable it may be, but it's a distribution circuit if it's anything at all."

Fritz scowled. "Are you sure you didn't lose it and pick up another cable in error?"

"Do me a favour!" said Jacko. "We were feeding a signal

into the thing at the switching house and picking it up all the way down the cable. I tell you that thing is a distribution complex originating, not terminating, at the subway building."

Fritz sat up sharply. "Distributing power where?"

"I hate to tell you this, but it covers a fair proportion of the Southern plain. The cable divides and sub-divides *ad-infinitum* as far as we can tell. We counted divisions into roughly forty thousand pairs and that still left a fair majority—but we gave up when we found what was at the end of a dozen or so of the minor pairs. I'll give you three guesses . . ."

"Don't tell me," said Fritz. "I can imagine . . . ruddy great Tazoon harps."

"Harps, harps and nothing but harps, and never a string between them. Listening to music I could understand, but can you seriously maintain that they installed five thousand million loudspeakers across the plain just so that they could listen to the trains? Nobody could be *that* alien!"

Fritz thumped the table. "Jacko, you're a ruddy genius!"

"Am I?" Jacko blinked.

"Yes. You've given me the clue I needed. Get the squad together, Jacko, we're going to re-start the subways of Tazoo."

Ten weeks of the precious three months of Colonel Nash's ultimatum had elapsed before they were in a position to make the preliminary tests. The intervening period had been one of furious activity for the U.E. personnel, and one over which Fritz had draped a veil of secrecy such that nobody outside of his group had any idea of the direction of his slowly unfolding plans. But on the final evening everything was ready. Fresh cables of Terran newness threaded their way out of the subway entrance; and on the platform two dozen floodlights illuminated the mechanical achievements of a culture which had passed two million years before, and shone into the tunnel to light a vehicle which had stopped in that position at the same time that on Terra elephants were native to the Sussex Downs and the evolving ancestors of man had yet to distinguish themselves from their animal counterparts.

Shortly before sunset Fritz and his team assembled at the subway building. Already the calm stasis of the day was beginning to tremble with unease as the riding cloudrace overhead broke lower, heralding the nightly windy torment of the land. This was no lull before the storm but an increasing tension, a tight coil being further tightened to the inevitable breaking point which was the lash of the sand-filled gale. As the storm broke they hastened inside.

Fritz found himself more than slightly in awe of the thing he contemplated doing. Immaculate as was the preservation of these Tazoon artifacts he could not help remembering, as an engineer, the patterns of low temperature creep, the grain growth, the diffusion—all the degradation of properties which fabricated metals might be heir to after two million years of rest. Fortunately the Tazoons had understood their materials and their atmosphere well, and apparently had built to last, with a success which was phenomenal.

In any case, Fritz was now committed. Sentiment and curiosity apart, the very continuance of the U.E. depended on his ability to re-activate the subway. He could not draw back now even though the whole place threaten to crumble about his head in a welter of dust and thunder.

As was his custom when there were unavoidable risks to be taken, Fritz alone attended the array of instruments set up in the subway proper. Jacko was in the switching gallery on the other end of the communicator, in a hastily conceived control set-up which included the rest of the relevant monitoring instruments they had been able to piece together from the inadequate supplies brought to Tazoo. Jacko, uncomfortably aware of the danger of Fritz's position, had sought to dissuade his superior from being present for the actual test run, but Fritz, foreseeing the cataclysmic damage to the installation which might result from the experiment, had decided to be present to gain first-hand experience of the principles of operation which might by their own employment become hopelessly obscured.

Five minutes to zero hour, and Fritz took a last check on his instruments. He had already signalled Jacko to begin preliminary switching when he heard footsteps and voices echoing in the corridors leading to the platform. He snatched up the communicator.

"Hold it, Jacko. I think I've got company. Do nothing until you hear from me."

"Right," said Jacko. "But it's none of our boys down there, I promise you."

"No," said Fritz, "but unless I mistake the gruff undertones it's Colonel Nash and his aides. I'll have to get rid of them, of course. We'd get ourselves a bad name if we knocked off all of the top brass in one go." He slammed

down the handset and marched up the platform just as Nash
and his retinue arrived.

"Lieutenant Van Noon," said Nash icily, "I have just been
informed of your intention of trying to re-start the Tazoon
subway this evening. As this is a project of the first magnitude
I think I should have been more directly informed."

"You will be, sir, as soon as we have anything to report."

"I don't think you quite appreciate my point," said Nash.
"If you succeed in this it will be the very first Tazoon mechanical artifact of any moment to have been re-started. As
such it is a rather—er—historical occasion. Naturally I'd
have liked to have been asked to be present."

"And I don't think you quite appreciate my point," said
Fritz. "There comes a point in the progress of any project
which is usually obscured by a notice reading: *Danger, Engineers Testing*. As far as we know the Tazoon subway is intact and perfectly preserved. From an engineering point of
view there is no reason why we can't switch on the current
and have it back in operation as it last was two million years
ago."

"Well?" asked Nash ominously. "What's the problem
then?"

"Just this," said Fritz. "How do we know that what was
normal for the Tazoons is even remotely tolerable for us?
The power input for this one sector of the line is quite
fantastic by Terran standards. The Tazoons don't appear to
have been fools about the efficiency of power conversion,
so I can only conclude that Tazoon subway operation was
a pretty hectic procedure. When they throw the master switch
upstairs we shall have a sample of Tazoon mechanical environment in the raw. I don't want anybody down here at
that moment who isn't absolutely essential to the success of
the operation."

Colonel Nash snorted with irritation. "The best available
information to date indicates that the Tazoons were small-
boned, avian and somewhat fragile creatures. I am perfectly
certain that officers of the Terran Exploratory task force are
able to tolerate the conditions in a deserted subway every bit
as well as its former occupants. But if you happen to be so
unsure of your mechanical aptitude why don't you switch
things on a piece at a time?"

"Because," said Fritz, "as far as we can tell the whole
system is interlocked back to a master computing house of
such complexity that it will take all of ten years to unravel

the individual controls. For reasons best known to themselves the Tazoons did not appear to have been in favour of local circuit isolators, so we have to accept the whole or nothing at all. I'm making a formal request, sir, for you to leave. If you remain I can't be responsible for the consequences."

"Are you staying, Lieutenant?"

"Yes, sir."

"Then we stay too. I appreciate it's your show, but I think you're over-stressing the danger angle."

"Very well," said Fritz. "But remember it was your decision." He returned wearily to his communication point. "Jacko, prepare to switch on."

"Have they gone?"

"No, they insist on staying to see the fireworks."

"Ouch! I hope you know what you're doing."

"If I did," said Fritz, "the chances are that there's nothing on Tazoo which could persuade me to stay on this platform while you throw that switch. Bring the current up to a maximum over thirty seconds and hold it there for three minutes. If you can't contact me on the communicator immediately you've switched off again then get down here fast with all the emergency equipment you've got."

"Right," said Jacko. "And good luck! I'm giving you a count-down of ten . . ."

SEVEN

If Fritz Van Noon was prepared for the worst experience of his life he was still unprepared for the sheer intensity and quality of the impressions which assaulted him. The whole tunnel cavity lit up in a kaleidoscope of lights of unbelievable colour-range and brilliance. The air grew rapidly and uncomfortably hot and choking with acrid vapours which his lungs could not accept and which burned his skin like the breath of a playful blowlamp.

But it was the noise that dug furrows in his soul. A series of rising screams from a dozen mechanical throats passed up through the audible range and into the low ultrasonic, causing dust fires to break out at intervals along the platform. Devices hammered and clattered and chattered in a cacophony which clawed at his eardrums with red-hot needles. Literally every fragment of the installation vibrated or resonated or contributed in some way to the atmosphere of screaming, explosive thunder. Ominously, the train which Fritz had stationed himself to watch, held motionless for a full minute then discharged itself in a rumbling, grinding ricochet into the station and down the further tunnel, accompanied by a cataclysmic roar which contained all the acoustic qualities of a continuous collision with an unending series of cheap tin tea-trays.

Scarcely had the first train disappeared from view than another skeleton juggernaut hurled itself upon the station and drove a hectic and furious path straight down the line and was gone before his senses could properly interpret its arrival. Fritz cringed before the shock-wave of its passing and watched his precious monitoring instruments scatter in all directions. He ground his teeth in mental pain at the sound of the mechanical anguish of tortured metal biting into tortured metal. Sparks and white-hot fragments showered the platform and peppered his coverall with a pattern of small singed holes.

Colonel Nash and his entourage were now crouched against the wall further down the platform, white-faced and with their hands over their ears, while some noise-making instrument above aimed horrific noises at their heads. Under their feet the dust smouldered with a repulsive miasmatic odour, reminiscent of kakodyle and mercaptan, which had to be smelled to be believed.

Before Fritz had time to realize the smile that blossomed in his bosom yet another train entered the station, this one fighting to halt itself with a spine-chilling screech of unseen brakes which fought valiantly to kill the horrible momentum. Fritz gritted his teeth and watched its progress right to the last shuddering halt. With his monitoring equipment out of action he was forced to estimate the vehicle's speed mentally and make a rough guess at the forces which would act on the passengers of a vehicle involved in such a drastic reduction of speed. The answer told him more about the physiology of the Tazoons than Nevill had deduced in the previous twelve months.

Abruptly the power died and his eyes were forced to adapt to the relative dimness of the Terran floodlights. His ears still whistled and ached from their recent battering, and the intolerable heat and humidity made him feel like the occupant of some outlandish turkish bath. Colonel Nash climbed unsteadily to his feet, a perfectly unreadable expression on his face, and picked his way carefully around the heaps of smouldering dust on the platform. His aides, lacking his aplomb, openly betrayed their relief at the end of the ordeal and hastened to the exit.

Nash made straight for Fritz.

"Van Noon."

"Sir?" Fritz saluted briefly while trying to balance a previous audio-frequency spectrum analyser which was in danger of falling off the platform into the channel.

"I owe you an apology," said Nash. "Lord, that was ruddy awful! But you've given me grounds for thought. I'm not saying you didn't warn me—but where in hell did you get all that power?"

"I'll be reporting on that, sir, as soon as I've tidied a few details."

"Very well," said Nash. "There'll be a Staff conference at three o'clock tomorrow in my office. I'd appreciate your answer then."

He turned and strode off, while Fritz became aware of the communicator buzzing urgently.

"Fritz, are you all right?"

"Only just," said Fritz. "It was grim. Everything was at least five times as fast as its Terran counterpart and about twenty times as noisy, to say nothing of the heat. If that's a sample of a deserted Tazoon subway in operation I hope I never have to suffer one during the rush hour."

"I've got news for you," said Jacko. "We had switching trouble up here on the temporary lines we rigged. According to our calculations we were only able to supply forty-three per cent of the total estimated loading. If you'll hang on for a moment I'll give you a test run at a hundred per cent loading."

"Don't bother," said Fritz hastily. "For that I'd need some repeaters and telemetry equipment plus a few unattended TV cameras. I'm not staying here for a hundred per cent loading run."

"Did you discover anything?"

"Enough. Initially the potential weakness of this system will be confined mainly to its passengers. The Tazoons were apparently using an adaptation of an A.C. linear motor for traction, with the bottom of the channel as the reactive element. On the same principle they use A.C. magnetic flux repulsion to lift the train clear of the ground so that they're virtually hovering on a magnetic flux field. I suspect the same principle should be operating on each side to centre the train with respect to the tunnel walls, only we didn't have enough current to make it fully effective. Come to think of it, it's a damn clever idea, with the train held in a mechanically frictionless supporting field with only inertia, air-resistance and eddy-current losses to be overcome by the traction system. I can't yet see how the current pickup is arranged, but that's probably inductive too. Suffice it to say we can soon adapt it to our own purposes."

"Good," said Jacko, "only I can't see that by so doing we're going to produce what we set out to achieve. They asked for a transport system and we're offering a subway with all that connotes in the way of limited routes and limited points of access. How long do you think that is going to satisfy Nevill?"

"For at least a lifetime, I should think," said Fritz. "The building of a subway is a climactic achievement in the history of any culture, requiring, as it does, the co-ordination of a considerable quantity of technological resources. Ergo: you only build subways to connect points which are sufficiently important to warrant such endeavour. Give Nevill a functional subway under this city and he will have immediate and convenient access to all those points of the city which the Tazoons themselves thought worth while making accessible. You not only have a transport system but a considerable pointer to the psychology and cultural habits of the Tazoons themselves."

When Fritz arrived at the Staff conference he had the feeling that the rest of the meeting must have been convened about an hour earlier, for the assembly was already engaged in earnest discussion at the time of his arrival. Nevill was leafing forlornly through a formidable pile of notes, reading abstracts, and Colonel Nash was in the chair.

"Ah, Lieutenant, take a seat. We hope you are going to tell us how you came by that impressive source of energy which enabled you to put on that display last evening in the subway."

"I can do more than that," said Fritz. "I think I can add considerably to our knowledge of the Tazoons themselves. But let us start with the harps—Tazoon harps. I suddenly realized what they were."

"And what was that?"

"Mechanoelectric energy converters—piezo-electric generators, if you like. The harps are merely assemblies of high-efficiency piezo-electric crystals operated by the vibrating strings of the harp. The strings are made to vibrate by the passage of the Tazoon night winds."

"I'm no scientist," said Nash, "but I would have thought that piezo-electric effects were scarcely of sufficient magnitude to be useful for energy conversion on that scale."

"A common misconception," said Fritz. "Even our relatively undeveloped Terran ferroelectric ceramics are capable of something better than a power generating density of sixteen watts per square centimetre, which has solar cells beaten hollow. The Tazoon crystals are capable of an output of eighty watts per square centimetre and a conversion efficiency of better than ninety-five per cent, an efficiency markedly better than even the most advanced Terran M.H.D. oscillating-plasma reactors. Mechanoelectric conversion has always been a highly promising line of development, but hampered by the fact that on Terra there was a scarcity of large-scale sources of mechanical energy of useful frequency. The Tazoons made ultra large scale use of medium-level energy by utilizing the winds to activate the harp strings. A Tazoon harp in a typical night wind is capable of an output approaching two kilowatt. This comes out to around a megawatt of power for each square kilometre of plain equipped with harps."

"Are you sure of this, Fritz?" asked Nevill.

"Perfectly sure. We powered the subway by re-stringing some of the harps out on the plains there."

"But doesn't the output vary with the force of the wind?"

"Yes, but with the harps ranged over a wide area the variations average out fairly well."

"But how did they obtain their power when there was no wind?"

"They didn't," said Fritz. "We've found nothing which would indicate any attempt to store the power nor any suggestion of an alternative supply. When the wind stopped, everything stopped. Thus by habit if not by nature the Tazoons were probably nocturnal."

"But this is ridiculous," said Nevill. "I still can't conceive that they would fill whole plains with electrical generating transducers."

"Why not? They had no particular use for the great outdoors. By and large their native environment was intolerable to them."

Nevill sat up sharply. "That's a highly speculative statement to make. How do you arrive at that conclusion?"

"Simple," said Fritz. "Firstly, they were nearly blind, hence the need for such inordinately intense lighting such as we found on the subway. If my calculation is correct even Tazoo at mid-day was a pretty dull affair to their eyes. Secondly, the temperature the subway reached was so far above ambient that it's a reasonable guess that they couldn't tolerate outside temperatures for very long. They had a very low body mass and presumably chilled rapidly."

"Incredible!" said Nevill. "I knew they were small-boned, but body mass . . ."

"If you'd seen the rates of acceleration and deceleration of a Tazoon subway train you'd soon see that only creatures of small body mass could survive it."

"All right," said Nash, "you seem to have all the answers. Perhaps you also know why the Tazoons become extinct?"

"I could make a good guess. Even more than ourselves the Tazoons were power dependent animals, for the aforementioned reasons. They had reached a point where they couldn't exist without power for light and heat, having presumably reached an evolutionary dead-end which had put them out of phase, so to speak, with their native environment. Now remember that they depended on power from the harps, not having any great resources of alternative fuels, either fossil or nuclear. Remember also that the harp frames were made of ironwood from the trees of the forests which used to adorn the plains. I suggest they increased their power generating areas at the expense of the trees until at some point they encountered soil erosion. Normally soil erosion is reversible if the right steps are taken to combat it, but . . ."

"Well?" said Nash.

"Soil erosion led to sand and the sand and wind conspired to form a sandblast which abraded and destroyed the strings of the harps. The failure of the harps meant loss of power— the very power essential to bring in the purified sea-water necessary to help combat the soil erosion. The process developed into a vicious circle—more sand, less harps; less harps, more sand, and so on *ad-infinitum,* every day the situation worsening as the sand robbed them of the power they needed to combat its formation. When the sand grew deep enough it even prevented ironwood seeds from rooting, so the rest of the forests gradually died also. The Tazoons, faced with a gradual but unalterable loss of power, took the

only course open to them—they tried to migrate to the
tropical regions where the climate was life-supporting without the need for power. History seems to record that very few
of them ever got there, which is not surprising when you
consider that the night-wind was certainly capable of blowing a Tazoon clean into the air."

There was several moments' silence. "And the harps?"
asked Nash. "That was their sole means of power generation?"

"We have found nothing which would indicate otherwise."

"What a pity! Philip Nevill had just succeeded in per-
suading me to lend support for a rather ambitious project.
Consequent upon your demonstration of both power produc-
tion and a potential source of transport, Philip was proposing to re-establish the Tazoon city, initially to cater for
archaeologists interested in extra-terrestrial work, but later as
a permanent colony and as a supply base for ships moving
out to the Rim."

"You mean to re-populate the place—turn it back into a
living city?"

"Given time, yes. If possible also irrigate the deserts and
reclaim some of the wasteland. It's a great pity you have
such admirable reasons why it can't be done."

"But it can be done," said Fritz. "Given time and sufficient labour to repair the harps there's enough energy out
there to power the whole city and a dozen others."

"But I thought the sandblast . . ."

". . . ruined the harp strings. Yes, it did . . . but that was
before the advent of Fritz Van Noon. The Tazoons probably used a plain metal wire, possibly titanium, which was
susceptible to abrasion. Remember they had no organic
chemistry to speak off hence no plastics. We're using a high
tensile and extremely tough steel wire and a polysilicone
elastomer coating over it, which is a highly abrasion-re-
sistant combination and should give many years' service without trouble. Unfortunately it damps the vibrations considerably—but then, we don't need the degree of either heat or
light which the Tazoons found necessary."

"And you really believe the Tazoons became extinct because of the lack of a suitably coated wire?"

"Yes," said Fritz, "just that. And let it be a lesson to ourselves. We don't know what factors in our own technology
may be lacking when it comes to meeting some new and

unexpected crisis. Our development is probably as one-sided as the Tazoons, but in another direction. Therefore nothing but benefit can come from the complete assimilation of every phase of Tazoon science and technology into our own. If colonization can do that, then I'll see you have the power to colonize."

"For the want of a nail . . ." said Nevill speculatively.

"Fritz," said Nash. "I've been meaning to speak to you about the possibility of permanently establishing U.E. as a branch of the Terran Exploratory task force instead of merely a section of the Engineering Reserve. How would you react to that? Of course, it would mean promotion. . . ."

"I should personally welcome the idea, sir," said Fritz, "but I fear I've already accepted another assignment on Tiberius Two. They're trying to establish a mono-rail system there."

"I see," said Nash. "And just what is there about a mono-rail system on Tiberius Two that requires your peculiar talents?"

Fritz coughed discreetly. "I understand it's something to do with their gravity. Apparently it changes direction by seventy degrees every Tuesday and Thursday morning," he said, reaching for his cap.

The Fiend

by

FREDERIK POHL

Celebrated for his excellent short stories and novels during the past two decades—and biting satires in collaboration with the late C. M. Kornbluth—American author Frederik Pohl occasionally departs from the accepted path of science-fiction storytelling and, as in this latest story of his, presents it from an entirely different angle . . . a long spaceship voyage with a cargo of colonists in suspended animation—and a captain whose mind dwells on a dream from his earlier youth.

How beautiful she was, Dandish thought, and how helpless. The plastic identification ribbon around her neck stood out straight, and as she was just out of the transport capsule, she wore nothing else.

"Are you awake?" he asked, but she did not stir.

Dandish felt excitement building up inside him, she was so passive and without defence. A man could come to her now and do anything at all to her, and she would not resist. Or, of course, respond. Without touching her he knew that her body would be warm and dry. It was fully alive, and in a few minutes she would be conscious.

Dandish—who was the captain and sole crew member of the intersteller ship without a name, carrying congealed colonists across the long, slow, empty space from Earth to a planet that circled a star that had never had a name in astronomical charts, only a number, and was now called Eleanor—passed those minutes without looking again at the girl, whose name he knew to be Silvie, but whom he had never met. When he looked again she was awake, jack-knifed against the safety straps of the crib, her hair standing out around her head and her face wearing an expression of anger.

"All right. Where are you? I know what the score is," she said. "Do you know what they can do to you for this?"

Dandish was startled. He did not like being startled, for it frightened him. For nine years the ship had been whispering across space; he had had enough of loneliness to satisfy him and he had been frightened. There were 700 cans of colonists on the ship, but they lay brittle and changeless in their bath of liquid helium and were not very good company. Outside the ship the nearest human being was perhaps two light-years away, barring some chance-met ship heading in the other direction that was actually far more remote than either star, since the forces involved in stopping and matching course with a vessel bound home were twice as great as, and would take twice as much time as, those involved in the voyage itself.

Everything about the trip was frightening. The loneliness was a terror. To stare down through an inch of crystal and

45

see nothing but far stars led to panic. Dandish had decided to stop looking out five years before, but had not been able to keep to his decision, and so now and again peeped through the crystal and contemplated his horrifying visions of the seal breaking, the crystal popping out on a breath of air, himself in his metal prison tumbling, tumbling for ever down to the heart of one of the 10,000,000 stars that lay below.

In this ship a noise was an alarm. Since no one but himself was awake, to hear a scratch of metal or a thud of a moving object striking something else, however tiny, however remote, was a threat, and more than once Dandish had suffered through an itch of fear for hours or days until he tracked down the exploded light tube or unsecured door that had startled him. He dreamed uneasily of fire. This was preposterously unlikely, in the steel and crystal ship, but what he was dreaming of was not the fire of a house but the monstrous fires in the stars beneath.

"Come out where I can see you," commanded the girl.

Dandish noted that she had not troubled to cover her nakedness. Bare she woke and bare she stayed. She had unhitched the restraining webbing and left the crib, and now she was prowling the room in which she had awakened, looking for him.

"They warned us," she called. " 'Watch the hook!' 'Look out for the space nuts!' 'You'll be sorry!' That's all we heard at the Reception Centre, and now here you are, all right. Wherever you are. Where are you? For God's sake, come out where I can see you."

She half stood and half floated at an angle to the floor, nibbling at imperceptible bits of dead skin on her lips and staring warily from side to side. She said, "What was the story you were going to tell me? A subspace meteorite destroyed the ship, all but you and me, and we were doomed to fly endlessly towards nowhere, so there was nothing for us to do but try to make a life for ourselves?"

Dandish watched her through the view eyes in the reviving room, but did not answer. He was a connoisseur of victims, Dandish was. He had spent a great deal of time planning this. Physically she was perfect, very young, slim, slight. He had picked her out on that basis from among the 352 female canned colonists, leafing through the microfile photographs that accompanied each colonist's dossier like a hi-fi hobbyist shopping through a catalogue. She had been the best of the lot.

Dandish was not skilled enough to read a personality profile, and in any event considered psychologists to be phonies and their profiles trash, so he had to go by the indices he knew. He had wanted his victim to be innocent and trusting. Silvie, 16 years old and a little below average intelligence, had seemed very promising. It was disappointing that she did not react with more fear.

"They'll give you fifty years for this!" she shouted, looking around to see where he could be hiding. "You know that, don't you?"

The revival crib, sensing that she was out of it, was quietly stowing and rearming itself, ready to be taken out and used again. Its plastic sheets slipped free of the corners, rolled up in a tight spiral and slid into a disposal chute, revealing aseptic new sheets below. Its radio-warming generators tested themselves with a surge of high-voltage current, found no flaws and shut themselves off. The crib sides folded down meekly. The instrument table hooded itself over. The girl paused to watch it, then shook her head and laughed.

"Scared of me?" she called. "Come on, let's get this over with! Or else," she added, "admit you've made a boo-boo, get me some clothes and let's talk this over sensibly."

Sorrowfully Dandish turned his gaze away. A timing device reminded him that it was time to make his routine half-hour check of the ship's systems and, as he had done more than 150,000 times already and would do 100,000 times again, he swiftly scanned the temperature readings in the can hold, metered the loss of liquid helium and balanced it against the withdrawals from the reserve, compared the ship's course with the flight plan, measured the fuel consumption and rate of flow, found all systems functioning smoothly and returned to the girl.

It had taken only a minute or so, but already she had found the comb and mirror he had put out for her and was working angrily at her hair. One fault in the techniques of freezing and revivification lay in what happened to such elaborated structures as fingernails and hair. At the temperature of liquid helium all organic matter was brittle and although the handling techniques were planned with that fact in mind, the body wrapped gently in elastic cocooning, every care exercised to keep it from contact with anything hard or sharp, nails and hair had a way of being snapped off. The Reception Centre endlessly drummed into the colonists the importance of short nails and butch haircuts, but the colonists were not always convinced. Silvie now looked like a dummy on which a student wigmaker had failed a test. She solved her problem at last by winding what remained of her hair in a tiny bun and put down the comb, snapped-off strands of her hair floating in the air all about her like a stretched-out sandstorm.

She patted the bun mournfully and said, "I guess you think this is pretty funny."

Dandish considered the question. He was not impelled to laugh. Twenty years before, when Dandish was a teenager with the long permanented hair and the lacquered fingernails that were the fashion for kids that year, he had dreamed almost every night of just such a situation as this. To own a girl of his own—not to love her or to rape her or to marry her, but to possess her as a slave, with no one anywhere to stop him from whatever he chose to impose on her—had elaborated itself in a hundred variations nightly.

He didn't tell anyone about his dream, not directly, but in the school period devoted to practical psychology he had mentioned it as something he had read in a book and the instructor, staring right through him into his dreams, told him it was a repressed wish to play with dolls. "This fellow is role playing," he said, "acting out a wish to be a woman. These clear-cut cases of repressed homosexuality can take many forms . . ." and on and on, and although the dreams were as physically satisying as ever, the young Dandish awoke from them both reproved and resentful.

But Silvie was neither a dream nor a doll. "I'm not a doll," said Silvie, so sharply and patly that it was a shock. "Come on out and get it over with!"

She straightened up, holding to a free-fall grip, and although she looked angry and annoyed she still did not seem afraid. "Unless you are really crazy," she said clearly, "which I doubt, although I have to admit it's a possibility, you aren't going to do anything I don't want you to do, you know. Because you can't get away with it, right? You can't kill me, you could never explain it, and besides they don't let murderers run ships in the first place, and so when we land all I have to do is yell cop and you're running a subway shuttle for the next ninety years." She giggled. "I know about that. My uncle got busted on income-tax evasion and now he's a self-propelled dredge in the Amazon delta, and you should see the letters he writes. So come on out and let's see what I'm willing to let you get away with."

She grew impatient. "Kee-rist," she said, shaking her head. "I sure get the great ones. And, oh, by the way, as long as I'm up, I have to go to the little girls' room, and then I want breakfast."

Dandish took some small satisfaction in that these requirements, at least, he had foreseen. He opened the door to the washroom and turned on the warmer oven where emergency rations were waiting. By the time Silvie came back biscuits, bacon and hot coffee were set out for her.

"I don't suppose you have a cigarette?" she asked. "Well, I'll live. How about some clothes? And how about coming out so I can get a look at you?" She stretched and yawned and then began to eat.

Apparently she had showered, as was generally desirable on awakening from freeze-sleep to get rid of the exfoliated skin, and she had wrapped her ruined hair in a small towel. Dandish had left one small towel in the washroom, reluctantly, but it had not occurred to him that his victim would wrap it around her head. Silvie sat thoughtfully staring at the remains of her breakfast and then after a while said, like a lecturer:

"As I understand it, starship sailors are always some kind of nut, because who else would go off for twenty years at a time, even for money, even for any kind of money? All right, you're a nut. So if you wake me up and won't come out, won't talk to me, there's nothing I can do about it.

"Now, I can see that even if you weren't a little loopy to start with, this kind of life would tip you. Maybe you just want a little company? I can understand that. I might even co-operate and say no more about it.

"On the other hand, maybe you're trying to get your nerve up for something rough. Don't know if you can, because they naturally screened you down fine before they gave you the job. But supposing. What happens then?

"If you kill me, they catch you.

"If you don't kill me, then I'll tell them when we land, and they catch you.

"I told you about my uncle. Right now his body is in the deepfreeze somewhere on the dark side of Mercury and they've got his brain keeping the navigation channels clear off Belem. Maybe you think that's not so bad. Uncle Henry doesn't like it a bit. He doesn't have any company, bad as you that way, I guess, and he says his suction hoses are always sore. Of course he could always louse up on the job, but then they'd just put him some other place that wouldn't be quite as nice—so what he does is grit his teeth, or I guess you should say his grinders, and get along the best he can. Ninety years! He's only done six so far. I mean six when I left Earth, whatever that is now. You wouldn't like that. So why not come out and talk?"

Five or ten minutes later, after making faces and buttering another roll and flinging it furiously at the wall, where the disposal units sluiced it away, she said, "Damn you, then give me a book to read, anyway."

Dandish retreated from her and listened to the whisper of the ship for a few minutes, then activiated the mechanisms of the revival crib. He had been a loser long enough to learn where to cut his losses. The girl sprang to her feet as the sides of the crib unfolded. Gentle tentacles reached out for her and deposited her in it, locking the webbing belt around her waist.

"You damned fool!" she shouted, but Dandish did not answer.

The anaesthesia cone descended towards her struggling face, and she screamed. "Wait a minute! I never said I wouldn't——" but what she never said she wouldn't, she couldn't say, because the cone cut her off. A plastic sack stretched itself around her, moulding to her face, her body, her legs, even to the strayed towel around her hair, and the revival crib rolled silently to the freezing room.

Dandish did not watch further. He knew what would happen, and besides, the timer reminded him to make his check. Temperatures, normal; fuel consumption, normal; course, normal; freezer room showed one new capsule en route to storage, otherwise normal. Goodbye, Silvie, said Dandish to himself, you were a pretty bad mistake.

Conceivably later on, with another girl. . . .

But it had taken nine years for Dandish to wake Silvie, and he did not think he could do it again. He thought of her Uncle Henry running a dredge along the South Atlantic littoral. It could have been him. He had leaped at the opportunity to spend his sentence piloting a starship instead.

He stared out at the 10,000,000 stars below with the optical receptors that were his eyes. He clawed helplessly at space with the radars that give him touch. He wept a 5,000-000-mile stream of ions behind him from his jets. He thought of the tons of helpless flesh in his hold, the bodies in which he could have delighted, if his own body had not been with Uncle Henry's on coldside Mercury, the fears on which he could have fed, if he had been able to inspire fear. He would have sobbed, if he had had a voice to sob with.

Manipulation

by

JOHN KINGSTON

The psi powers of the mind—telepathy, telekinesis, teleportation—have offered wide variations of plot in recent years, from such outstanding novels as Wilson Tucker's Wild Talent *in 1955 to the more recent* The Silent Speakers *by Arthur Sellings. New author John Kingston presents a rather macabre plot of a man gifted with one of the psi qualities and slowly developing a second—but such talents can be dangerous.*

No!

No! No! No!

I said I would never use my Power again. I won't. It's wrong and vile. I remember what I promised myself ten years ago, walking in the dark after Mother died.

It kept her alive for years. The doctors had never seen anything like it. It was her heart. . . .

God knows it was difficult. Not like this thing I want to do now. This could be so easy.

When Mother was alive I used to stay up nights, work round the clock on that feeble old heart, strengthening, renewing. I built a new valve once, piece by microscopic piece. Three days and nights that took me, working nonstop. Do you know how many cells there are in the ventricles of a human heart?

"I do. . . .

Mother knew what was happening. She could feel all the little adjustments going on, the million cobweb-forces twitching between us keeping her alive. She tried to give up three times. But she couldn't die because her heart couldn't stop. And her heart couldn't stop because I was driving it.

Technically she did die once. I worked that heart for twenty hours before it would beat on its own again. They'd use an electronic pacemaker now. There was nothing of the sort then.

I was born with my Power. It didn't seem wrong to use it. I couldn't sit and let her die. I never realized though until almost the last, how she'd come to hate me. Hate my phosphorescent eyes and my million hands, tiny, invisible, never-resting hands. . . .

I pull the bedclothes over my head, trying to make the black room even darker. I dig my face in the pillow, try to shut out the deep noise of the overrun as Julie changes up after a corner. But I only succeed in muffling my ears.

Mother had won in the end. She was too clever for me. If she'd cut her wrists or opened her throat it wouldn't have mattered because I'd have seamed up the wounded flesh as fast as the blade went through it. If she'd jumped from a building I'd have caught her and lowered her to the ground. But she didn't do that. All she did was swallow a hundred little white tablets.

I woke in the night. I was already inside her. I knew what was wrong. Knew she'd beaten me. I was fast enough to juggle cells as they multiplied and died, but these were molecules. The wrong sort of molecules. They came pouring and flooding through the universe of her body, changing things as they came. I could see amino acids and peptones, watch proteins building up like pearly chains against a void, but now there were too many molecules. I fought them, I was everywhere at once, grabbing them, altering them, making them harmless. But it was no use. It was like a locust plague. Like trying to catch the insects one by one in your hands and kill enough to stop the swarm, and the sky dark with them for miles. . . .

I had to walk out from inside her, leave everything still and quiet. I ran away from the house, using my feet. I never went back. Since then I've never used the Power. I won't now. I've been hungry, and not used it. Sat in a cell and unlocked and locked the door the long night through. It was only a poor steel thing, useless and simple, and I played with it, but I wouldn't help myself. My Mother killed herself to get away from this . . . thing I can do. I won't ever use the Power again.

You can look up telekineticists in books. They'll tell you they are people who can move things without touching them, change physical states at a distance. They'll also tell you such beings don't exist. Well, the books are wrong.

I'm one. . . .

I ram the heels of my hands against my eyes. Peacocks flick their tails beneath the lids. The nervelights paint Julie in crazy colours, lilac and aniline red and burning green, but they can't block her out.

She's driving a wheeled rainbow. The colours lap and flow along the bodywork, stream out behind the tail. I relax the pressure and the iridescence vanishes. She is still there.

I can't help it. I have a million hands again, groping over that flying car. I'm low down in the chassis, in the springs, feeling the shocks stream into the tempered metal. Watching the curving rush of the road, looking out through the stoneguard with the white fans of the headlights in front and the geometric cliff of the rad behind me. I'm in the engine seeing in spite of blackness the clamouring ballet of pushrods and tappets. In the steering column feeling the stresses from the wheels, the countering resistance of Julie's arms. I linger at the steering rim, savouring the transition from metal to flesh where her hands are gripping it firm. . . .

I feel my pulse accelerating. That pounding, that isn't the engine that's my heart. I go rigid, not breathing, thinking of what I'm going to do. I poise two of my hands over her wrists, others above the roaring venturis of the carbs where I can see the throttle linkages move in unison as she drives through the bends. In a second I'm going to whip her arms behind her, pinion them, open the throttles and take control. I'm going to watch her face as the silver road snakes at her and the trees, as the revs climb and the wheel-rim in front of her swings to the bends. Faster, and faster, and faster . . . and when she's had enough, when she can't take any more. *I'm going to let go.* . . .

I roll out of bed and slap at the lampswitch with my hand. My face and body are covered with sweat. I run the tap in the handbasin, put my head under it. The cold water shocks. I glare round. See double. The details of the tawdry room registering dim through flashing, white-lit trees. The noise of the engine, its drumming in my ears. I reel about, put my hand out to the rushing macadam that is a wall. I know I've got to break this link. I concentrate, put all my being and will into it. The images I want form somehow. Putting out an oilwell fire. Reeling fuse, waiting, pressing the plunger . . . *Now* . . . a huge flash, obliterating everything. . . .

Silence. Dimness. A little room in a cheap boarding house. Faded, striped paper. Useless gasbracket draped with cob-webs. Cracked mirror. My jacket, trousers, slung across a chair. I'm leaning against the wall trembling. I go sit on the bed. Light a cigarette, drag the smoke down deep. This is better. I'm O.K. again.

I don't think I'm just a telekineticist.

God, listen to me! *Just* a telekineticist. . . . It's true, though. I've got this other thing, E.S.P., psi factor, devil possession, I don't know what its name is. To . . . do a job, I don't even have to be there. I can walk through a city miles away, see the neon and the crowds, alley cats prowling, leaves and cigarette packets in the gutters, rain bouncing on the roads. I can watch a murder done there, or an act of love, and have to go find a nameboard to see where I've been. . . .

Distance is nothing to do with it. Near or far, it's all the same. For instance right now I know Julie's driving a car. But I don't know where. She could be a mile away. She could be in Nevada.

I think about something else, anything. I don't want to go back to Julie for both our sakes. I pull on the cigarette. I get mad. I ask myself, what do books and names matter, what the hell's a name? Nobody like me has ever existed before. I've got a wild talent.

The room is quiet as a grave. I finish one cigarette and light another from it. I still feel shaky. I get up, go to the cupboard over the washbasin. It's a flat-brown, rickety little cupboard, fluff and muck on the top of it, badly fitting doors. I scraped a bit of paint off a door once. It wasn't wooden. Made out of bits of Victorian newspapers stuck together to make a sort of cardboard. Next the cupboard there's the mirror, one corner gone, glass flecked over with greasy ginger spots. That's the sort of trash I live with. And I could have made my fortune.

I open the doors, get out a bottle of Scotch and a glass. I pour myself a treble and put the bottle back. Suddenly the room seems stuffy, full of smoke. I go to the window, undo the catch. I bang the grimy frame to free it and lever it open. Cooler air moves against my face and there's the noise of the main road just down the hill. I lean on the sill and stare at the moving reflections of the lights. The road roars like that all night long. Julie's on a road right now, driving somewhere. God knows where.

Something wakes up in my mind. It's like stepping on a dog you didn't know was there, seeing it come up at your face. It's as quick as that. For a second I'm seeing the bonnet of a speeding car, hearing an engine louder than the ones outside. I jerk back into the room in panic. The car vanishes. I realize how careful I've got to be.

I lay back on the bed with the glass in my hand. I start to make up a mental image. Something I can hang like a screen in front of the thing I don't want to see. I compose the picture all of opposites. Julie's car is rushing along, doing eighty or ninety. So I take something static. A rock will do. It's a red car so we'll have a neutral, blue-grey sort of rock. The car's moving in darkness, so my rock will be in pouring sunlight. Yes, there it is, big and blue. Immensely static. Deep shadows round its base where it's embedded in the ground. It's a good sharp image; I can see the striations in the rock and the weathering, feel the sun heat striking back from it on to my face. I stand back mentally, appraise my work. Yes, that'll do, it's fine. That rock won't ever move.

The roomlight starts to annoy me, glaring in my eyes. It's a naked bulb on a flex, no shade. Yellow crab-patterns from the filament reaching across the ceiling. I put my hand out and switch it off. I don't need light any more.

I finish the whisky and go back to my rock image. I recognize it now. It's a rock I saw when I was on holiday with Bill years ago. There's that little bay behind it and the sun-haze, the twinkle of the sea. I remember that holiday well, little bits and snatches of it are so clear. How old would I have been? Nine, ten? Something like that. I try to work out how long it's been since I saw my brother. Must be all of six years. Old Bill was a good chap. Hadn't got my . . . gift, lucky blighter.

He knew about it though. That's why we're estranged. . . .

I think back to that holiday, evoke as much of it as I can. The cigarette makes a steady arc in the blackness as I draw on it, let my arm sag to one side, draw on it again. The sun-glint on the water, hot sand, the tallness of cliffs. Coolness and hardness of their great flanks turned away from the sun, suck and boom of the sea in the hidden caverns at their bases . . .

Julie has gone on holiday. Down to the coast with Ted to laugh and kiss and lie in the sun and show off her body. . . .

The whisky starts to take effect. I feel dopey and confused. I'd had a good thrash before I came up tonight. I'm with Bill again but he's not sitting on the rock, he's driving it. It's red, it has headlights and it roars. The road slips away behind it . . .

The cigarette bites into my fingers. I fling it away and lie back again. My hand throbs. But I don't bother to mend the burn. I'm glad of the pain. It keeps me within myself, lying on a bed in this rooming house, safely. I lie for an hour, watching the moon rise over the rooftops, hearing the cars on that distant road. I sleep. . . .

It's a hollow, confused sort of dream. There's Julie, face underlit from the dash, eyes big and soft-looking in the light from the dials. The wind gusting through the lowered driving window, playing in her hair. Short hair, gay-unruly, curly, copper-brown. She's a redhead, but not green-eyed. Deep blue eyes, aquamarine. Dark now, solemn. She's concentrating on the road. She's a good driver. I can feel how good she is by the responses of the machine. She's not riding that motor, she's a part of it. The wheels, the gears, they're extensions of her body. I crane round for a look at the speedo. She's holding a steady eighty, keeping it up mile after mile. No effort. I wonder where the hell she's going in such a hurry. This wasn't scheduled . . . I wonder about the car. It isn't hers, I'm sure of that, and it couldn't belong to Ted. It's just a fine motor, not flashy, not chromy enough for Ted. Not showy enough by half.

I don't worry long. In dreams, you just accept. . . . I watch the road whipping under the bonnet, streaming out behind the clean line of the tail. After a time I get to feel the car's stationary, the wheels just idling, keeping pace with the flying ground. Then I seem to see the whole earth rolling under those wheels, the car fixed in space but still leaping towards the rising sun. I feel myself whirling with the planet, the tug of gravity urging my body down towards the deep core. I begin to lose all sense of identity. . . .

A road sign goes past but I'm not quick enough to read it. I move restlessly on the bed, conscious of doing wrong, too sleepy to pull out of the dream again. I start playing with the steering.

This is fun. I'm holding the car's wheel, hard, opening my grip and letting the rim slide to the bends, feeling Julie's strength take the motor round. Then grip again, relax, grip . . . if she wanted to move that wheel now she couldn't because I've got it braced; she couldn't move it a fraction, I'm stronger than she is——

Damn——

"Oh, I was too late then. A hundredth of a second was all but I was still too late. I should have known, she's got such a touch . . . she felt the wrongness there in the steering column. She knew there was something. . . . A sudden tug, unexpected, trying me out. My hands were away and gone in a flash but she felt the resistance. I saw the frown come, in the same instant I let go. She's testing again now, cautiously, little pulls one way then the other. But the wheel is free. . . .

I sit up slowly. A second ago I was nearly asleep. Now sleep is a million miles away. I was never so awake, so cold. I . . . felt something then. Only for a moment, but it was there. A little surge of feeling, the first start of panic. *And it wasn't my fear.* . . .

I try to swallow; but my mouth, it never had any saliva. It's bone dry, desiccated, feels raw. I find the cigarettes. My hand is clumsy, spills them over the bed and across the floor. I feel for one in the dark, light it, flick the match away. I lie there with the thing in my fingers, drawing on it and seeing the glow reflect back ghost-pink off the ceiling. My body is quiet, but not my brain or my heart. The heart thuds steady, savage; I can hear the thumping in the silent room. I'm . . . intensely alive, head to toes. My body feels everything, knows everything. I can sense the earth turning again and myself spreadeagled on it inching towards the sun. . . .

That's what I meant about Mother hating me. Right at the last, when we were fighting like that, me wanting to keep her and her trying to go away and down, I felt her mind. That's how I know. The hate, it was like a bright flame scorching at me then getting dimmer, flickering, dying away. . . . No words. They're nothing. . . . It was worse than words. Later, when the shock had gone a little, I wanted to do it again, make a contact with somebody else. But I couldn't. The telekinesis, that was no trouble ever. It refined itself and sharpened, got more and more sensitive even though I'd left it lie to rust. . . .

I know why my heart is protesting like this. It's because I realized subconsciously in that split part of a second when I was touching Julie's mind that this other thing has been growing in the dark as well. I know now I can do it again. I know I'm going to be a telepath.

And they don't exist either. . . .

I go back, deliberately this time, to the car. I feel as if I'm moving along a predestined course that can have only one end. I study Julie in microscopic detail.

She's driving slower, not much above fifty. She's still testing, veering in to the verge then back out to the cat's eyes again. Pulling and touching at that steering, trying to account for what she felt. I don't know what's in her mind. I strain to make a contact but there's nothing there. She centres the wheel and accelerates. I catch a tiny shrug, the smallest lift of an eyebrow. She's decided she dozed for a moment. She'll have to be more careful. She's been driving a long time and she's sleepier than she realized.

They weren't her thoughts, they were mine grafted on.

I know when I'm in another mind; there's . . . something. Everything. Colours and textures all different. A new way of breathing, thinking. Impossible to get it into words. It's weird. You own another body, another soul. . . .

I've got to be careful here. I can't be sure, but I think she suspects me. . . . I meddled with her once you see. A long time back. It was late at night and I was drunk. She felt the incubus, I'm sure she knew it was me. It didn't do any good, and afterwards it gave me hell. . . .

I lie there a long while trying to rest. My heart is still pounding away under the bedclothes. I move my hand down and feel it bumping at my ribs like something trying to crack out from an egg. I know, in a detached way, my body won't stand this strain for ever. Something will have to give. . . . Somehow or other I've got to resolve this thing. Then I can relax.

First, I've got to beat the fear.

There are a lot of sorts of fear. I suppose one sort comes if you're on your own some place and you cut an artery and there's nobody to help and you know you've only got minutes. That's fear . . . and another sort is when there are the footsteps in the night, and the creaks and the laughing, and the branch taps the pane, insistent there behind the curtains; but there isn't any branch. . . .

I'm about to enter another mind. That's the worst fear of all. . . .

I've done it before, but only seconds at a time. And then it was bad enough. This is going to be worse than opening a private diary, packed full of things about you. Worse than looking in a mirror under a glaring light. Worse than these things, more truthful than the diary, more searching than the light. I begin to see the only thing that keeps any of us sane is that we can't communicate. Oh we can talk, write letters maybe or compose music, a poem, they're better ways of getting across, but we still have to be tuned and nobody's ever finally certain what the message is. . . . We're all in a mist, thick, like cotton-wool. We hide in it from each other, from ourselves, wrap ourselves away. Deep down we want it like that because it's for the best. . . .

But there's a devil inside us, we call it hope. That last little thing the girl let out the box, that was the worst plague of all. It's hope makes you ask the question when you already know the answer, hope makes you open that locked diary, turn on that glaring light. . . . I don't want to hope, I'm through with it, done. But I'm hoping. . . .

I try to steady my heart but my own body's out of control. I turn my ears inward, hear the blood move like water pounding through a weir. I realize I'm gasping for air and somehow make my breathing slow down. . . .

I can see now, all my life I've been moving towards this one point. I'm going to do something now that nobody's done before. I'm going to develop, shake out my wings and soar. I'm going to do it because it has to be done. No other reason's big enough. This will be a turning point in the history of the world, the first event in a new order of things. It's going to happen here, in this damp, peeling attic room. Well, a man can't always choose the place and time.

But why Julie; God, why does it have to be with Julie?

Got to stop thinking like that. I tell myself I don't matter. I'm dead, dust. . . . I try to see the bigness of what's going to happen, the panoramic significance of it. For a few moments I almost manage it. It isn't exactly like a vision; it's like standing on the edge of a great sea and hearing the bawling, confused noise of it and knowing it stretches away and away for all time. . . .

Once there was a primal cell. It hung in a void and it was complete and perfect, it *knew itself*. . . . But the cell had to split, and the halves sailed away, and there was mystery. And the mystery grew, through all the years stacked on years that we call Evolution. . . . There were people, groping in the mist, trying to know. . . . Man and woman, the woman wanting to enfold, the man wanting to lose himself, go right back down to that primal core, that oneness. That's the only peace we look for till the grave. Nothing in life but needing to join; and that's a need we share with everything that ever lived right through time. The soul passing to Nirvana, that's the state of not-being, of union with everything, ultimate rest . . . the gods will die at the Ragnarok, all things cease at Armageddon . . . not-being is fusion, fusion not-being. I see the whole shape of evolution, complexity increasing, the old cell running and jumping and crawling and slithering and oozing and flying, then gliding back, recombining into a unit all-seeing, all-knowing. The return to the monobloc, the end of mystery. Here, in this dirty room in a two-bit town, that reversal is about to start. Two entities go back to oneness. The cell that split all that dumb time ago knows itself again. . . .

This is it now. Go steady, boy. You're uplifted, outside yourself. You've left self behind. Nothing matters except that you go steady, go slow, *make your base.* . . .

I can see her face again in the light from the dash. Her eyes, mouth . . . little beauty spot on her lip, her teeth, hair curling against the collar of her windcheater. I never paid even Julie this close attention before. I feel I'm getting closer to the thing I want to do. . . .

Surprise.

I know dimly the way I'm going to manage the jump. How to get across into the other half of perception, the part they call telepathy. It's a sort of—twist, a piece of mental acrobatics. There's no basic difference between this and what I could do before. But I thought . . . never mind. Let it go, it doesn't matter. Sort it out later. The end counts now, not the means.

I was trying too hard before, thinking there was a difference. It's still a case of grasping something at a distance, it's just that I've never tried to hold anything as nebulous as this. Like catching a will o' the wisp. I retain the physical picture of Julie, as clear and sharp as an image in a stereoscopic film, and I keep . . . moving forward is the only way I can describe it, edging after that Jack o' lantern Thing that doesn't quite have a form. Julie's thought. . . .

I'm getting a clear picture through her eyes. That's something I never quite managed before. I realize arbitrarily how good her sight it. We watched the flick-flick-flick of the cat's eyes in the road. Our minds are very close now. She's half hypnotized by the winking studs. So am I.

Deeper again, nearer. . . . Back on the bed my body has stopped breathing. I'm almost home. Somewhere a thought forms. *"Been a long night."* Another answers it. *"Yes, but the night is nearly done. . . ."*

Her thoughts?

No, mine. Both mine. . . . There's one of hers though. In the mist. Mist? Fog. Void. Primeval. . . . It's iridescent, with a texture, a resistance of its own. Impossible to hurry here. Like swimming under water. Nightmare, seeing the thing ahead, not able to move. Don't know where I am. On the border of things physical . . . inside an atom. . . .

It's easy, at last. The thought, the thing that fills her mind; it's there right ahead, opening like a flower. I'm stationary, not pushing any more, swallowing fire that doesn't burn. . . .

A click. A lens dropping in some complex array. Final adjustment . . .

Reflex. A leap, a gurgling flailing convulsion that takes me out of her, body and mind, with a cold wrenching, leaves me falling, a hundred miles up, no parachute, the ground spinning up to meet me as I come right back down to earth——

I'm lying in the little room. There seems to be a weight on my chest, pressing me down. My stomach is full of quicksilver or lead; something heavy and cold and final. A taste in my mouth, rusty, salty, like blood. Heart pounding still but slower, heavier. All effort done.

There was feeling there. A rushing sense of love, a compound of sorrow and pain. And an image, vague at first and shaky like something seen through water then hardening and taking on form and colour, becoming recognizable . . .

Ted, grinning up at me out of the depths of Julie's brain.

I hold a hand out in front of me in the darkness, slowly clench it into a fist. I open the fingers again and see the white half-moons on the palm darken and fill. The blood trickles down to my wrist. I don't make a sound.

I try to remember what I was thinking about a few minutes ago. It's cloudy now and vague. I'd been going to change the course of history hadn't I? Achieve something of cosmic importance, reverse evolution. Give God a bit of a helping hand, solve the Mystery of Life. How completely can you fool yourself? I'm not going to solve anything. Or achieve anything. I see I was putting off the moment when I had to poke into Julie's mind because I was scared of what would be there. I never wanted to change the universe. I only wanted one thing. Julie. It's more than a want now, it's a burning, a huge need. But I can't have her. I know that finally, from what I saw in her mind.

I'm nothing. I never was anything. Telekinesis, that's a toy for kids. I can see that now. We've all of us got telekinesis, we've had it for years. We can all move things miles off, look into closed boxes, see round corners. Well can't we? We've got machines can do all that for us, all that and more, telekinesis isn't new any longer. And the other thing, what good is that, it can show me how people hate, despise. . . . I can see myself in their minds bloated, obscene, a reflection from a Hall of Mirrors. . . . I don't want to see myself like that, painted garish colours by

Julie's fear and loathing. I don't want to see her sublimated vision of Ted. I don't want anything any more.

Just that short time ago my Power was the reason for existence. Now I don't want the Power. There's nothing left. No point in going on.

I lie there a long while under the weight of that snippet of knowledge. Then, slowly at first, I begin to see the wild humour of the thing. I start to chuckle.

I roll my head backward and forward on the pillow. I can see myself now as a sort of cosmic clown, shaking my unearthly cap and bells. The image is hilarious. The laughter gets louder, bubbling out of me. I realize the noise is ringing in the little room. I try to stifle it. I hold my breath; for a time I quiver inside then I get calm again.

I still have a decision to make. It isn't the decision I thought it was though, it's something quite different.

Suddenly I remember a guy I used to know years back. Lorimer was his name, or Latimer. Yes, that was it, Eddie Latimer. Good-looking guy with a sensitive dark face and the sort of strong thin wide-knuckled hands you see on an artist or a craftsman. But he was beat, way down. He was a sculptor, or had been, and he drove a dumper for a living, and all the hate there ever was showed there in the backs of his eyes. We used to swill beer together in some town or other, I've even forgotten the name of it. And he only ever had one message for me. "Hate" he used to say. "Hate is O.K., it's the same as love. Insignificance, not-mattering, that's the only thing that's all-out bad. If you can't be loved son, *be hated. . . .*" He'd done some black things, had Eddie, in the name of hate. . . .

There isn't a decision any more, it's been made for me. I'd been going to use the Power for good, take a step forward that maybe folks everywhere would have learned to copy. It was a big experiment, I didn't mind being the guinea pig. But the first thing I saw embedded in Julie's mind, the image of the grinning gigolo she picked out for a mate . . . I couldn't take that, I wasn't expected to.

So it looks like this is the Will of God. . . .

Nothing that breathes can ever really stop still, only in death. And I'm not going to kill myself. I can't stop using the Power now, I can't build for good so I'll build for evil. Just like Eddie. I can't be loved so I'll be hated. *I will not be mocked. . . .*

Now I need the stimulus of rage. I could reach into myself and milk my own adrenals, set them pumping. But I won't. I'll do it the slow way. That's better because you can feel the power inside you build up and up. That way there's a consummation.

I go back in time to just after Mother died. I parade all the empty days, the effort, the hopelessness.

Like I said, I gave up telekinesis. I owed that much to her. But I was smart. I used the other thing instead, the harmless watching ability. I'd got a plan for myself.

Right back from when I was a little kid I knew what I wanted. Money, and the power it gives you. I was going to make sure nobody would push me, work my guts out, break me like they broke Mother. I saw her get old trying to run the family, keep us fed. That's the way it is in this life. You either burn up other people or you get burned up yourself. Mother got burned up. Maybe she was happy in a way. I don't know and I don't care. All that matters is they burned her up. I had to watch it. I used to tell myself whatever else came, that wasn't going to happen to me.

The things of this world. . . . Like a mug I thought I could get them. Even without the Power. All I had to do was take a job, any job. And wait. Follow people about, the way I can. Meet their pals, listen to them talk business. Follow them into the bars, into the shut offices where the big deals are made. Overhear them planning then forestall, move out on my own. Buy the land the Supermarket needed, snap up shares when the price was rigged to climb. . . .

But it didn't work out.

The world's a big place. Take any city, any town. Did you ever try watching a thousand people at once? Did you ever try *listening* to them?

I'll tell you about it. It's like a sea. It's like a sea and you drown. You can't take it. It's meaningless. You hear snatches, scraps. They jazz about in your mind, just on the edge of making sense. Then you lose the pattern and the thread and you open out a little more and in comes a tidal wave of voices and you drown. . . .

In the end I found out how to select. I could tune my brain and pick up anybody anywhere and hold them like I was holding Julie. I learned a lot then. I always knew where ten notes would make fifty or a hundred would breed a thousand. And you know what? I didn't have those notes. Not the hundred, not the ten. And you can't make money without money, did anybody ever tell you that or did you find out yourself the hard way? In the old days I'd have stood outside a bank, close up by the night safes, and the thousand notes would have come rustling up the chutes into my hands, but the old days were gone. I'd given up the Power.

There was another thing. That got me worst of any.

I had a boss once. Big man. I used to call him sir. And it was yes, sir, and no, sir, please, sir, and thank you, sir, day after bloody day. Until I—followed him home. Saw the little castle. Saw how the wife handled him when nobody was around. Then I knew why he was a big man all his days. Because he was a cringing thing all his nights. . . . And after that the yes, sir, no, sir, it wouldn't come any more. So I got out. . . .

I was working with a guy once on a machine. Two of us on that one big machine all day long. He was a nice quiet guy. I used to go and drink with him odd times. He was a nice guy. Used to talk on soft and low about all the evil there is in the world, about wanting to bring in some goodness when he could and live in peace. Well, one night I followed him as well. With my mind. He'd had a few drinks, I wanted to see he got home O.K., that was all. . . . But he didn't go home. He crossed over some waste lots, and prowled, and waited. He found himself a little school-girl, out too late alone. . . . So I moved on. Because after that I couldn't work the machine with him any more, or drink with him or treat him like a nice guy. . . .

It was always like that. And there were the little people round me pushing and scrambling, and the great gift I couldn't use, the thing I couldn't even talk about because they'd have taken me and strapped me in a cell. . . . Do you know what loneliness is, or frustration? I knew what Eddie had felt like while he worked that dumper, while those strong artist's hands of his pulled levers and twisted throttles, and the machine hauled muck from one place and tipped it in another. . . .

Then I met Julie.

I remember the first time I saw her. It was in this town, a couple of years back. I was making pin money slinging beer in one of the locals. It was summer and the air was hot and heavy and sweet. It was Festival week and the bars were full, skiffle bands playing, everybody going a bit crazy and letting down their hair. She shouldn't have noticed me.

Girls like Julie just don't see the guy who hands their drinks. But she saw me. Those eyes . . . I can remember her like it was yesterday, standing laughing in the smoke and brightness. But her eyes weren't laughing. They were watching, calm and deep, and anything you wanted to believe, if you looked in those eyes, it was there. . . .

I saw her again. When I wasn't working. Maybe I was crude about it. Maybe I was brutal. She didn't care. I got myself a little joke of a car and we used to go about in it, drive somewhere and find a quiet place to have a meal or go way out in the country, just sit and listen to the trees. And she'd watch, and talk, and it was right. I knew it. Just right. Until Ted moved in.

At first I didn't believe it. I thought I knew you Julie, I really did. I tried to joke about it once, remember? Only you wouldn't laugh. You said "He's nice. I like him, we have fun." And the way you accented that last word, just enough. That word went through me like a knife, just how it was supposed to. And then you watched me, carefully. You waited to see how I'd react. . . .

Even after that I kept trying to think it was some sort of game you were playing. His face started to haunt me. I can see that damned face now. Pale and triangular. Heavy-framed glasses. And that smooth dark sweep of hair over the temple. Oh don't forget the hair, the college-boy status symbol. And the eyes. Almond shaped and tilted and leering, always leering, gloating at me. Even the way he walked, that was an insult. He used to walk like an animal. Swing those thin hips somehow, I don't know how . . . there was something there that was like an animal. But that was what you wanted all along wasn't it?

Wasn't it?

He was a car salesman. When he wasn't selling cars he was driving them. Great rangy cars, the sort of machines I could have owned just by stretching out my hand. . . . They were the things you really wanted, weren't they? There was the night you let him dice me, all up the road and down. You were sitting with him and your hair was blowing and you were waving and grinning at me clattering along in my old Ford Eight. That was your big night Julie, do you remember that?

Maybe it wasn't your fault. The way I feel now I could nearly be sorry for you. I thought there was something deeper in your mind. I thought under all the laughing you

were like a kind of little waif straying about looking for
something a bit better than kicks. It wasn't your fault I
was wrong. . . .

I only realized after I lost out how much you'd got to
mean. I couldn't see anything any more but the back streets
and the rain, misery and coldness stretching to the
end of time. You'd put the years and the frustrations away
from me somehow. When I was with you it was like they
never happened. But now all the pain was back, and I didn't
know how to keep going. . . .

But from now on in, things are going to be different. Tomorrow I'm going to lift myself a couple of hundred in old
untraceable notes and some ready cash in silver. Then I'm
going to start working on it. And by the end of the month
I shall have a couple of thousand, Julie, and in two months
I shall have ten, and an alibi nobody will break, not if they
try for years. Then I shall have a car, just like the cars
you want, and clothes like the clothes you expect to see on
your men. And I shall have women and wine and there will
be songs but I won't be singing them any more. And I shall
go on, and go on, and I shan't ever stop. You hit the deto-
nator, Julie, and the bomb is going off, and it's the biggest
damn bomb anybody ever set off in this sweet world. It's
going to be a beautiful explosion.

But there's just one thing. *You won't be alive to watch
it.* . . .

You didn't know I could kill, did you? Neither did I, up
until a few minutes ago.

The Rage!

It wants to get free now and tear and maul and run red-
handed in the streets. But I'm holding it back because I've
still got to be careful. Later on, when they all know there's
a new god on the earth, it won't matter. . . .

I wish I could invite an audience to watch this. The world's
only telekinetic engineer is about to give his first real demonstration. I'm going to kill a false thing called Julie, because she put shame on me. And shame I will not bear. It
won't be a very pleasant death. It isn't supposed to be.

This has got to look like an accident. I could kill abruptly,
finish her like you might dispatch a rabbit, but I don't dare.
Not yet awhile. There are just a few people who suspect
me. Eddie was one and there was my brother, I don't
know how much they understood. . . . Somebody might see
a news item in a paper, put two and two together. They

might ask themselves, what breaks a girl's neck in a speeding car then floats out through the crashing metal un-
harmed . . . and they might guess. Then the word would get
out, the whisper in the dark, *mutant* . . . and you'd come for
me with death in your hands, I know you humans when
you're scared. . . .

I'm moving my fingers forward and back along the chassis
of Julie's car, examining every projection, every bolt. I'm
looking for a weak link, some unit I can take apart so it'll
look like it fell to bits on its own. I think of the brakes.
I work my way from the foot pedal down to the master
cylinder under the floor, along the hydraulic lines where
they twist through the chassis and out to the hubs. I don't
want to touch the master cylinder, that would look too obvious, but the unions on the slave cylinders are a possibility.
Undo one of those nuts and the fluid would spout free
when she touched the pedal, there'd be no braking action
at all. But I'm not certain she'd crash. She's a great driver
and she'd still have the handbrake and the gears. She'd feel
the sponginess in the pedal as soon as the line started to
bleed, she'd get stopped somehow. This has got to be something that makes the motor uncontrollable the instant it
comes adrift. Like a tyre burst. I wonder about the tyres
but there's no quick way of weakening a tread.

I watch Julie's face for a moment. I get sick. I ask myself, why did she have to choose that second to be thinking about Ted. . . . I don't give the idea a chance to develop. How do I know how many hours a day she spends
drooling over him? Tune in any time, the call-sign's always
the same. . . .

I move away again thinking about fire. I have a look at
the tank end of the fuel-gauge system. No chance there,
the thing's cased in too well. I could make a spark but it
wouldn't touch the vapour. And anyway petrol's queer stuff,
won't always burn just when you want. I come back along
the chassis, hang in the noisy space under the scuttle and
watch the acceleration torque tilting the engine, the road-
springs flexing in front of me. This isn't as easy as I reckoned.

The car's a huge complex machine and there's a monster
riding it, soaked away in the very pores of the metal, but
the monster is nearly helpless. I can't break an axle, I'm not
that sort of superman. And I've realized I daren't touch Julie,
the fingers would leave marks, it would look bad. . . . I'd

like to get a wheel off completely but even that might not do what I want. You shed a roadwheel at ninety it isn't healthy, but your car doesn't necessarily lose balance all at once. You plane along till you slow down, then your brake-drum drops and you spin, but chances are even whether you spin off and crash or whether you just spend a kinetic fortune tearing up the road metalling. And anyway I can't get hold of the wheelnuts. You work out the trajectory of one of those nuts when the car's moving, you'll find it jumps along in a series of ellipses like a high-speed grasshopper. I can't hold a nut when it's acting like that. . . .

Something moves under my hand. I focus downwards and I have my answer. Under the bonnet the steering column ends in a bulky steering box. The roadwheel assembly connects to it via a drop-arm that's held in place by a castellated nut. I take a mental cross-section of the unit. If that nut came free nothing could stop the drop-arm riding down the splines and falling clear. You couldn't steer, Julie, with the linkage taken apart. And if you braked, with the front wheels running free. . . . There are a lot of things can go wrong with a car while you're driving. There are remedies for most of them. There's no answer to this. This is death. . . .

I take a long breath, and hold it. Then I find the split-pin that locks the steering nut in place, compress it with my fingers, draw it through the shaft and let it fall away. I expect the nut to start twitching undone. It doesn't move. I test it. Still tight.

Back on the bed my body frowns, bites its lip. I bring more strength to bear. No use. I put out full effort for a moment, relax with a grunt. The nut stays firm.

Julie slows for an intersection and suddenly there's a lot more traffic. I see signboards but I'm too slow to read the names. I leave the car and hurry back, but I get lost in the dark. I home on Julie and get on with what I've got to do.

I use a technique I developed once to deal with things like this. Normally I can't put out much more strength at a distance than I can with my bodily hands, but this does sometimes work. I place—that's as near as I can get to describing it—I place a pair of hands on the nut and grip it tight. Then I bring another pair into play at right angles to the first. Then another pair and another until I've got the shaft surrounded by a ring of force. The leverage is the same you get from a spider, one of those multi-armed socket spanners they use in garages. I wait, gathering strength. I twist.

A jolt from the road helps, the nut starts to turn. More than that, the drop-arm comes free on the splines. I gasp a bit and spin the nut loose. It drops off the end of the shaft, hits the road and bounds away. I'm afraid of it bouncing back and clanging against the chassis but it vanishes without a sound. That's good. . . . It's just the splines now holding the drop-arm to the box, and Julie's motoring as hard as ever. I ease the arm almost clear, nearly to the end of the splines, and hold it there. And I yell, a long noise that goes tearing down the night.

For not thine but mine . . . mine is the kingdom, and the power. . . .

Only an eighth of an inch on the splines now and the whole thing getting hard to hold. I hang on to it, strain to keep it in place while I have a last look at Julie. . . .

Julie damn you you can't do that. What are you doing——

I should have expected it. You were big and bold right up to the last minute when you knew you have to die then you remember you were a woman and the lashes of your eyes got salty and tangled and the tears ran down to your chin but it doesn't make any difference Julie, this is the jungle and we're the animals and you lost out because I was stronger than you thought. This doesn't figure, animals don't cry. . . .

The night and space splitting apart, laughter crackling among the spheres. Julie's holding the car at ninety down a black straight and she's crying and I was going to wipe her out like she was a bug on the wall but I can't do that while I can see the tears. They remind me she's real and she can be hurt and scared and her hair smells good and her body's strong and warm. I'm doubled up on the bed and there are two vibrating arms coming out of my mind to the steering box holding the link in place and I can't think any more. I only know this is Julie, I'm killing Julie, I can't do that . . . I can't hold the hate-image while I can see the tears, it's like trying to make a picture of water and see it run shapeless and drain away. I can see the crash now, eyes widening and widening and her mouth trying to scream and the metal fingers coming jagging in, opening her body like a red-silk rose. . . .

Julie this is Alan pull in Julie get off the road get off the road get off——

I think of something and act before the thought has time to finish forming, reach up and try to sweep the plugleads off the block, but I can't spare the power and the drop-arm jerks and I nearly lose it. I cram it at the box, trying to force it up the splines, and my body arcs off the bed but the link won't shift, I can only grip it and hold it where it is. There's something wrong, why won't the drop-arm go back on the splines . . .

No hand to spare for the ignition key. Nothing to spare. . . . My voice is yelling at Julie and there's somebody beating on the wall. I can see the window swirling about, the sky beyond it bright with the moon, shapes moving there against the stars. The shapes are in my brain.

They used to burn people at the stake for trying to do what I can do. Why can't I be like other people, they only go to bed to sleep . . .

I can't hold on too long at a distance, I never could. I'm still holding the drop-arm, but now it's like it was covered with acid, eating the flesh off my hands. The strain builds faster all the time. Plot it on a graph and you'd get an asymptote, because there's a quadratic involved in the basic expression and the curve swings up from the time axis towards infinity. . . . The stupid idea churns in my head and I try and find some clothes.

There's light showing under the door, somebody trying to get into the room. My body falls against the wall, stands up breathing a gale. Why am I trying to dress, it's all hazy. . . . The bit of me that can still reason is telling me I've got to try and close the gap between self and subject. I fumble with the doorlock, the key. . . .

There are stairs in front of me. Oblongs of light from open bedroom doors. Hands grab for me and I fight them, then I'm falling, holding the drop-arm, the hallway coming up to meet me. I land with my ribs across the stair-treads and the drop-arm slips and I think Julie, you didn't have to hit me so hard, why so hard. . . . I'm standing again but there are hot wires in my body burning the flesh as I move. I'm holding the linkage but my fingers are so weak now it's like trying to keep it together with pads of cotton-wool. Got to get closer to Julie, it sometimes helps. . . .

I fumble at the street door and it opens and there's a rush of night air. Then I'm running, with the fire banked up and crackling in my chest. You broke me up, Julie, the bones feel like they're swilling round lose inside me. . . . I stop at the corner, hang on a lamp standard, see flashes in the night the colour of spilled mercury, but the footsteps come rattling after me and I run again. Black buildings jerk past each side. I make the car park and weave across it in the moonlight and there's the old Ford by the wall. My mouth feels like' it's full of blood.

The keys are in the dash and I start up, holding the drop-arm. Julie, I'm sick. Why are you doing this to me. Get off the road. . . .

I accelerate and the people who were after me get out of the way somehow. The faces loom in the headlights and swing sideways and there's the gateway and I get through it with the tyres making a noise like something's dying under the wheels. There's the main road ahead and the lights. My foot is down on the boards and the Ford is roaring and stinking and I'm praying Julie, be out there somewhere, be coming towards me from the west, don't be going the other way. . . .

I can hear the banging as the suspension bottoms. Headlights sail at me and the cat's eyes stretch away wriggling and shining and I don't know where I am, I'm seeing through Julie's eyes again and I can't drive in six dimensions. . . . I swing to a bend and the bend isn't there. I crab back on to the real road and there's a blare of horns behind me and the long wild noise of brakes. I'm clocking sixty and the Ford's building up on a long slope and the bearings are yelling for mercy and I pray again, don't let her throw a conrod, sweet Jesus don't let her throw a conrod. . . . Two roads fork out from the windscreen and one is a hurtling ghost, but I can't shut it out. . . . I see an X-ray mess of images, the roads, the night, the drop-arm with the splined shaft locked through it, Julie, her hair, the tears. . . .

Can't you see where I am . . . my side . . . got to stop, lie on the grass, vomit out all the sickness and pain. . . . I ram at the brake, but the pedal feels solid and I'm in nightmare, the throttle is still pressing itself on the floor . . . I kill the ignition, but the key twists again under my fingers and the silencer bellows and the engine comes back to life and I feel like I'm choking, can't get any air. I yell, *Julie.* . . .

And it's like the sun came to meet me, putting out golden arms. . . .

The images she sends, I can't take them in. She's so happy, she splashes them out like a kid playing with water. She asks me, *Couldn't you tell? Couldn't you tell when you saw my eyes?*

I should have known. There were a thousand things should have told me. . . . When I felt her in the car, nobody could drive like that and be a part of the cogs and gears unless they were like me, I'm not alone any more. . . .

She makes a sea and it's golden and she wants me to go into it and sink down in the quiet and the cool to where the lights half blue and half gold, but I can't go into the sea because of the drag-link. . . . I try to tell her about the steering, but she swamps me. She sends laughter and it bursts inside me like the sun exploded. I've got my hands over my face trying to stop the brightness and the wheel is moving on its own and Julie's playing with me like a kitten with a ball of wool. . . . She sends the Ted image again and something comes jumping after it and catches it and Ted shrivels like a worm under a burning-glass. She knew there was somebody like herself and she thought it was me, but she wasn't sure and she had to be careful. . . . She used him to make me react, but I wouldn't move, I just let her go. . . . She left him and went home and begged her father's car and drove and drove to get back to me because she had to know for sure. And she felt me in the controls and she was happy, then she lost me and she started to cry because she thought I'd gone away. . . .

But I hadn't gone away, I was down there at the steering box getting ready to kill. . . . Julie, the steering box, get off the road. . . .

She asks me, what? What was that? Then there's a gasp and a scorch of rage and I know she's found the linkage and both our minds are down there holding it on the box, and she's trying to brake. . . .

The hands come off the Ford's wheel and I grab it and there are two roads, jazzing and swinging. I drive for the straight and then I know I'm wrong and there's a bend in front and I'm not going to take the bend. The car's bonnet dips under the brakes and she starts to swing and the trees are coming, growing out of the night, and Julie screams and the drop-arm falls off the box. . . .

Time, it's slowed right down. I shall have time to tell you about death. . . .

I feel the Ford bounce across the studs in the middle of

the road, see the surprised headlights as the oncoming traffic tries to get out of the way. I miss the first lights, but the second pair swing out to meet me and I know this is it. And I realize the Power that was given to us, it was too much for us to bear. The load was too heavy, we had to set it down. I'm sorry, Julie, I didn't want to make you cry. . . .

The thing that's going to kill me is close now, turning out to meet the Ford. The headlights glare but I can see between them and underneath. The light from a following car strikes through under the wheels and I see the useless steering link hanging down, dragging along the road.

There won't be time after all. I have half a second left to laugh. . . .

Testament

by

JOHN BAXTER

Young Australian writer John Baxter has a penchant for psychological stories with a gruesome outcome, if one is to judge from his published works, and "Testament" is no exception. On the other hand, you will agree that his story of a dying race's desperate search for food and water could not have been written effectively any other way.

I would rather not talk of this thing. There is in me the feeling I have had before only when I was in great danger, the feeling that the gods are angry and must be satisfied. Against their rage there is no protection. My mouth is dry when I think of this. My hands sweat and my body trembles. To talk of what has happened makes my fear worse, and I would rather remain silent. But the elders have ordered me to record what has been done, that those who come after may know and understand better. So it is set down here.

It begins in the last month of the year of drought. These were bad times. My family had not tasted real food for many weeks. We had only the dried seeds of grass and the little juice we could squeeze from plants. There was no meat or blood. Always we were thirsty. Even in the temples the sacred well was dry and young men going for their initiation were turned away. The elders told them to come back when there was again water in the canal. From the hot dark blueness of the sky, it looked like being a long time.

Finally, when our seeds were nearly used up, I decided to try hunting for sand lizards in the hills. It would be dangerous and the rewards would at best be small, but we were desperate. When it was hot and dry, the lizards mated, and at these times they were more savage than ever. Perhaps I would die—but why live if I must sit by while my woman and child die of starvation? After I had decided, I took down my spears from the wall and honed them. They would need to be sharp for the hunt.

In the morning I crept out of the village. It was cold and wet in the darkness. The dew settled on me like the touch of frozen hands. The huts huddled to the canal. Nothing stirred. Even my family knew nothing of my going, so there was no sound. This was the way I had wished it to be, but I did not turn my face to the desert without longing for a word of farewell, a wave, even the bark of a dog. It was as if I had already been given up for dead.

Out on the plain I began to run. That way, I could keep warm until the sun rose. It was easy going, even with my spears on my back, because the ground was still frozen. It rang like stone under my sandals and each time I put down my feet I could feel the crackle of frost. After a while I stopped and looked back. The village was hidden in its hollow. Now I was alone under the black sky, barely lit by the sun. It would be hours before it would warm to dark blue. But for the jagged hills in the distance, it seemed, the sky would settle to the plain and crush me. I pulled my furs about me and shivered. It seemed suddenly more cold. I took up my spears and went on.

By the time I had been running for an hour the sun was well up and the sky lighter. The black became a light purple and I knew it would be fine and hot. By the time I reached the edge of the hills it was hard to believe I had ever been cold. The sun beat down and my mouth was as dry as cloth. I thirsted for a drink; vegetable juice, blood, anything. Once I even found myself dreaming of water. It shocked me. I had not thought I would ever be that thirsty, nor that I could remember what water tasted like. The only time I had drunk it was at my initiation, three years ago, and yet out there in the desert my memory was as sharp as if it had been only yesterday. To help my thirst I sucked pebbles. If I found game, then would be my chance to drink deep. Only this thought kept me going as I picked my way upwards through the crevasses.

It took me another hour to reach the high places where the lizards live. There the world seemed to have been tumbled about by a demon. Around every turn there was a hole that could hide a dozen lizards waiting to leap out in a fury of fangs and claws. I undid the bundle of spears and checked them carefully. There was a heavy one with a sharp edge that my woman had made for me. The blade was beaten from a piece of metal she had found in the ruins. We both knew it would mean punishment if the priests found we had offended the law, but metal cuts better than stone and I had to be careful with the tools that brought my family food. So I carried this spear in my right hand, ready to thrust, and slung the rest on my back. Then I went in among the rocks.

I was very afraid, but I put my fear behind me and gripped the shaft tight. Fear would do me no good—courage might. It was my concentration on this that made me careless. I had been hunting for some minutes before I sensed the strangeness around me. I stopped and listened.

Many strange things then came to me. First, there were no lizards. The sun was hot and I knew I had moved too quietly for them to know I was there, and yet they were hiding, deep among the rocks. From what I did not like to think. There was no sound, only that of the wind whispering to the rocks in its own voice. Then, looking down, I saw that the sand on the path had been churned about by something passing by. Here and there in the confusion were hints of a pattern I had never seen before. My first thought was to run away, but then curiosity took me by the arm and I walked deeper into the maze, following the tracks.

It did not take me long to find the thing that made them. I came around a spur and almost ran into it. It was standing in the shade of a rock and, to me, it looked at that moment like a creature crouching to spring. I jumped back behind the rock, but the thing did not move and soon I saw it was not alive. I went closer. Still there was nothing. Now that I was near it, I could see this was no animal. It looked—though I know this sounds ridiculous—like a little hut on wheels. But such a small hut; my child would not have been able to get into it. And such wheels; they were small, but perfectly round and firm, far better than we could ever make from the scraps and splinters we have to work with. All around the house were clear openings filled with what I first thought was ice. But I touched it and it was warm and dry. This puzzled me, but I was too curious to think about it. I bent down and looked through the openings. Inside there were seats and strange tools filling almost all the space. And all so small. I wondered what kind of craftsman would make such a toy. Then a thought went through me like fire.

Perhaps a demon. . . .

I turned quickly and looked around with new eyes. Was I in a trap? In my fear it was not hard to imagine so. Any shadow could have held a monster, yet they were so deep in the bright mid-day that I would not have seen it. The silence was eerie. Only the wind moved among the stones. I leaned against the rock, listening. And soon I heard the sound of walking feet.

At first I thought it was a stone clattering in the rocks. But then it was louder, and I felt the regularity of it. Something was walking near me, very fast. I could not tell where. The echoes broke the sound into pieces and threw them all around me. I settled into a crouch. My spear, as if it too could hear, rose into the hunting position. We both waited. The steps grew nearer, louder. Short steps, hurrying to me. Closer—then suddenly before me their owner. I think I cried out in horror. Impossibly small, a strutting dwarf of a thing with one great eye glinting in its face. Before terror struck me down I threw with all my strength. The spear flew clean and sank deep. For a moment the creature clutched the shaft and tried to draw it out. Then, as if bowing to the will of the gods, it fell. There was no sound except for a hiss that died after a while. Where it came from I could not tell, though when it ended the body seemed fallen in on itself; empty and somehow more dead than anything I had ever seen. For a long time I waited, afraid it would rise again, but it did not move. As before, the wind talked to the stones. The sun shone.

When my body had stopped trembling I stood up and walked to the thing I had killed. It did not move. Would a demon move after being speared? I did not know. I walked closer. In death, the creature was less horrible. It sprawled like a discarded doll, legs and arms thrown out awkwardly. Only a stain of blood around the spear shaft showed that this thing had once lived. Now that my fear was almost gone, I could see things more clearly. What I had thought to be a single horrible eye was just a window of the same material as in the hut on wheels. And when I bent closer I could see something behind the window; something very like a face, looking up into mine.

Yet surely this was no natural creature. The body seemed like mine in many ways—the arms, legs, head—but they were all so small, like those of a stunted and deformed child. How could a chest like that draw breath? My own chest was three times larger around, and yet even I found it hard to breathe here where the air was thinner. I stood for a long time, wondering. The spear was like the marker on a grave, pointing straight up to the sky. Almost as a second thought I wrenched it out. And the blood flowed. When this happened my whole body seemed to burn. I felt for the first time the thrill of having killed. I remembered my dry mouth and the pains of hunger in my stomach. Perhaps I did wrong, but right or wrong I could not have acted otherwise. I took my drinking cup and drank deeply until I was no longer thirsty.

An hour passed. I lay by the rocks and slept. The sun was warm and even in the shade I needed no covering. Nothing disturbed my sleep. The only sound was of the wind and the sand it blew pattering against the rocks. When I woke, the sun was lower. Unless I hurried it would be dark before I arrived home. There was no longer any strangeness in the animal I had killed. I had drunk of its blood so now it was game and nothing more. Slinging it over my back I set out towards the village.

With food inside me, the going was easier. I almost ran despite my load, and sang an old hunting chant so loudly that even out there under the sky my voice rang. I walked into the setting sun proudly, thinking of a warm fire, a good meal, the faces of my people when they saw what I had brought. It was as good as I hoped. The children saw me first and ran shouting into the village. When I came down the path they were all standing in front of their houses, shouting a welcome. I swelled with pride. My chest was tight and I felt for the first time the triumph of a good hunt. In the centre of the village I dumped down my kill. The people gathered around. One of them, looking more closely, saw it was no ordinary animal. The others saw too, and were afraid, muttering among themselves.

But then I handed around a flask of blood I had taken from the animal. A few drank of it and, hearing their cries of delight, the others asked for a share. The mood of happiness returned. Perhaps we did not know what this animal was, but few people had ventured into the wild lands of the north and nobody knew what animals lived there. The house on wheels, the strange clothing, so much better than we could make—these we put out of our minds. It is easy to forget. We had starved long and were in no mood to throw the gods' gift of food back in their faces. When the elders had all tasted of the blood the women took the carcase away for preparation. A cooking pit was dug and spices brought out of hidden jars. It would be a great feast.

While we waited I sat near the fire talking with the other men, telling them over and over again of the hunt. This was real glory and I savoured it to the full while I could. But after a few minutes I began to feel ill. At first I laughed a little louder and forgot about it, but soon this was not enough. My body sweated all over and my stomach heaved within me. A moment later I was sick, racked with a retching that would not stop. Those sitting at the fire looked at me, then at each other, and their eyes were troubled. I pleaded sickness from the excitement of the hunt and slipped away to be alone for a while, but by then we all knew something was wrong and a fear was falling over us. Why had the blood made me sick? Why—unless it was unnatural food.

Shaking with fear now as well as sickness I went to where the women were preparing the food. I knew as soon as I grew near their circle that they too knew. They were not working. They had sung before—now they were silent. As I approached they moved away from the pit and I looked down at the creature I had killed. The tough clothing had been stripped away from the body and I saw the man within for the first time. All around me the women stood watching. Their eyes burned into my back.

As night fell, there were signs in the gathering darkness. We huddled before our huts, waiting. Beyond the hills there was a glow and a roaring of a fire more vast than any man can kindle. Then, just as the dark closed in, a thing came flying out of the sunset and bore down on the village. First it was just a dark speck against the sky, but then we saw that it was a terrible bird coming towards us, bigger and faster than any we had ever seen. And it flew more steadily than any natural animal. When it reached the village it circled as birds of prey do. It seemed to watch us, observing everything we did with a cold and unfeeling eye. We could not see it well in the dusk, but its shape struck a dreadfully familiar chord in us. We had all seen that shape before. It circled us for a long time until the last light was gone from the sky, and then it curved away and disappeared.

Looking around at the silent faces I knew they were all thinking as I was. The shape of the flying things was terrible like the rusted wrecks that littered the ruins. Out in the desert lay the hulk of some vast construction the function of which not even the elders knew. Littered around were broken containers long since worn to shreds by the desert winds. This was the place where a great bird had crashed to earth after bringing us from some other place—so the myth ran. But that was unimaginably long ago, before the oldest elder had been born, and there was nobody to tell if the tales were true. But I knew now that they were. And I knew too that the man I had killed had been a brother.

Now there is in my soul a great fear. The women have taken up the body and washed its wounds. He has been wrapped in his own clothing. The gashes in the cloth have been sewn up as best we can, but we all know it is not enough. The tears are like scars and they cannot be hidden.

The priests have raised the body high on a platform so that he may be near his home among the stars, and now they sit about him, chanting the prayers for the pacification of the gods. I have looked at the man I killed. His dead face stares up through the helmet at the sky, and in his eyes is a terrible yearning. He knows he can never go back to his home. And we too know that our homes will never be there for us to return to. Whatever happens, nothing will ever be the same again.

Now I have covered my body with ashes and put on the mantle of manhood. With the priests I will sit and sing the prayers and wait for judgment.

Night Watch

by

JAMES INGLIS

Not all science-fiction stories have to have human beings as the central characters, nor conversation and motivation to keep the plot moving. Here is a little vignette from the pen of another new British writer, with all the nuances of a Stapledonian epic packed into its few thousand words. In this case, not even the Universe is the hero.

With the instantaneous brilliance of a lightning flash, life and consciousness were born. The journey from void nonentity to vivid awakening was swifter than the passage of a meteor, instant and complete.

The search for self-identity began. Seconds after his awakening, the new-born being subjected his environment and himself to a minutely detailed examination. He discovered within himself, down in the misty centre of consciousness, a store of knowledge, all of it quite meaningless until linked with the stimulus of outside experience.

One thing he learned. He had a name. This was a convenient and necessary item. It was the symbol of individual identity. It defined the most important thing in his environment; himself. He knew that it would do more than that, he knew that his name contained the riddle of his existence. When he succeeded in interpreting this riddle, he would become aware of the purpose for which he was created.

Meantime, it was enough that he had a name. His name was Asov.

He turned his attention to the world around him, the baffling, incomprehensible world into which he had been born. It was a world of contrasts both glaring and subtle. Asov was at once sensitive to these contrasts and began to compare and measure, building up a picture of his environment on the fresh, fertile canvas of his experience.

Light and darkness. Motion and peace. Growth and change.

These were the concepts with which Asov wrestled, each new item of information being stored away within his miraculous memory and related to his inborn store of data.

The world took shape and meaning. His lightning senses could now instantly recognize a thousand variations in the interplay of energy which was how he saw the world. Like himself, the world too had a name. It was called Galaxy.

As he emerged from infantile bafflement, Asov could at last understand the riddle of his name. With that understanding came an awareness of his place in creation. His essential purpose no longer eluded him.

Asov. Automatic Stellar Observation Vehicle.

Suddenly, he became aware that one object in his immediate vicinity was demanding his attention, drowning out the innumerable distractions of pressure and radiation which were as sight and sound to him. The intensity of the object's attraction grew steadily, which Asov interpreted as meaning that he himself was in motion, and moving towards this blazing area of disturbance. This then was the source of his awakening. For a nameless time he had drifted in the void, a seed of dormant intelligence awaiting the signal which would melt away the cocoon of unconsciousness, the first, faint caress of light and heat which would activate his sleeping sensors.

The star registered itself in Asov's brain as a frenzied pattern of nuclear reactions and continuous explosions. This image he related to the pre-stored information within and translated the image into his creators' terms of reference. The star was a red dwarf, spectral class M5, surface temperature around 4,000° C. As he swung in a wide orbit around his stellar prey, Asov picked up the contrastingly faint light-heat emanations of smaller, cooler bodies which circled the dense old star in their timeless chains of gravity. He again related the incoming data with his inborn, encyclopaedic memory.

Planets: Four. Temperature range: absolute zero to near frozen. Condition: lifeless, having lost gaseous atmospheres. . . .

Painstakingly, unconscious of the passage of time, Asov continued his survey. When he was finished and his brain cells each held a full load of information, a signal was passed to his motor nervous system and with a sudden bound he was accelerating away from the domain of the red dwarf.

As the old star slowly receded, he completed the programme of his first mission. The data which loaded his brain cells was collated, coded and dispatched in a tight beam of radio waves, directed towards a tiny area of the firmament where lay the remote star Sol and the planet Earth. The planet which he had never known, but out of which he had come.

At last the urgency of his first stellar encounter grew dim, and Asov sought out the nearest available light-source, drawing upon the dormant energies of space to propel him towards his next encounter. Having completed the required manoeuvres, Asov drifted in the relative peace of the interstellar vacuum, where gravity came not in waves but in gentle ripples and the nuclear voices of the stars were no more than a faint chant, a cosmic lullaby. Asov slept.

The cycle was repeated each time he passed within the

gravitational embrace of any interstellar object capable of the slightest degree of energy output. The sources of his awakening-cycle were mainly stars of the red dwarf type, which comprised the bulk of the galaxy's population. But there were rare occasions when he would awake to the stimuli of massive giants and their proportionately enormous retinues of planets. Such occurrences demanded longer and more detailed survey, though of course Asov was unconscious of the time element.

Several times he passed through tenuous light-years of hydrogen, the life-stuff of the Universe. At times, these ghostly regions were sufficiently dense and luminous to wake his sensors, in addition to restocking his nuclear power reserves. Occasionally such nubulae contained the embryonic materials of new-born stars, hot and blue and amorphous. There was a great deal to learn at such times, particularly concerning the early evolutionary development of the stars. With each successive encounter his understanding of galactic processes increased, and was duly transmitted to the ever-more-distant point of origin.

Another rare event which Asov experienced was the discovery of a certain secondary characteristic of some planetary systems. The phenomenon of life. This characteristic was listed in his pre-birth instruction circuits as of the highest priority.

His first encounter with the phenomenon occurred while in the vicinity of a small, orange star of the classification G7. A star not unlike his native sun. He awoke to the familiar disturbance pattern; a strengthening of the gravitational tides which bore him, an intensification of light, heat and the full range of radiation. A new energy source was before him.

After the routine observations of the star, his attention turned to the solid bodies in orbit about it. Of these planets, two offered distinct traces of organic molecules. Even at a remote distance Asov's spectroscopic vision could wrest these planetary secrets with ease. For a more detailed survey, however, a close approach was necessary. Acting upon this preliminary data, his motor nerves were immediately stimulated to inject him into a planetary trajectory which would bring him into orbit about each of the target worlds.

It was the second planet which possessed the most rewarding conditions. First he noted the patterns of abundant areas of ocean. Spectroscopic examination revealed that the seas, like the atmosphere, were rich in life's constituents. Then came direct evidence of advanced life. As he swung in a close orbit around the planet, just clearing the violet, upper fringes of the atmosphere, Asov observed the unmistakable signs: lighted areas on the night-side, large artificial structures and courses, and most unexpected of all, contact. After many reconnaissance circuits he intercepted a stray tendril of radiation. A short analysis was sufficient to convince him that this could not be accounted for by the natural emissions from the planet. The only possible explanation was that the radio signal had been directed at him by an intelligence.

The Questor was being questioned!

In accord with his built-in responses, Asov returned a signal towards the unknown source on the same wave-length as the one he had received. This signal comprised a tightly coded account of Asov's home system, a record of terrestrial thought and history. In that small beam of signals was contained a thorough biography of man, his progress in medicine and philosophy, his discoveries and disasters.

Simultaneously, Asov was working on the message he had received from the aliens. This too was in the form of a mathematical code, which when broken down revealed a long and detailed history of two planets. Like man, the aliens were as yet confined to their local system, though unlike Asov's distant creators, they had evolved a global way of life which permitted world-wide understanding while encouraging the valid, essential differences between beings of even the same species.

On completion of the exchange, Asov passed on out of the kingdom of the orange star, quite unaware that he had been the cause of the greatest single event in the history of a solar system.

Although virtually indestructible in the erosion-free vacuum, and although his motive power was available in unlimited quantities from the suns and gases of space, there had to come a time when Asov would meet with unexpected danger. Normally his senses were swift enough to avert a likely collision. This danger was only met within the confines of a solar system, when passing through belts of asteroids and cometary debris, the coastal defences of the stars. Occasionally, these cosmic missiles would move at velocities beyond even Asov's power to out-manoeuvre. In the vicinity of large solar masses, the gravitational tides were so immense that much power was required for drastic course correction, and at the same time any local fleets of meteors would be moving with high orbital velocities.

It happened as he prepared to make his exit from the system of a red giant. The huge star had been a rare find indeed and it possessed the unusual feature of a retinue of minor stars, instead of the normal planets. These satellite stars were dwarfs, mostly in the last stages of stellar senility. They weaved around the sullen giant in weirdly eccentric orbits. So eccentric that the entire stellar system was a wildly turbulent whirlpool of gravitational forces. Enormous sized fragments of shattered planets flung themselves insanely across the system, as twigs will spin and dart in a vortex of water. Asov, given time, could have calculated precisely the mechanics of the whole complex system. He possessed the equipment to predict exactly the speed and trajectory of each hurtling fragment. But time, or the lack of it, was his undoing.

The collision when it came was not with one of the larger masses. These Asov had predicted and had taken evasive action. The fateful missile was a tiny splinter of rock, which compensated its insignificance in size with its vast velocity. It struck him at a point which in itself was expendable, upon a transmitting aerial of which he had several duplicates. But the shock of impact was great enough to deaden the sensitivity of his control mechanisms. In a coma almost as deep as death, Asov drifted helplessly into the dark wastes, unguided, aimless, totally without function.

It should have been the end. His inactive remains should have floated on for eternity, just another item of mineral debris in a Universe already familiar with the lifeless, the inert and the expended. But it was not the end.

In the furthest limits of interstellar space, as in the cosy realms of inhabited planets, the unexpected, the unpredictable occurs from time to time. Given long enough, and Asov had all of Time ahead of him, such an event was almost bound to happen. His was no immediate resurrection. He drifted in unconsciousness for the lifetime of many a star. While his senses lay dormant, planets formed, producing sea and slime from which finned oddities crept out on to cooling land surfaces to do battle with primal monsters and create civilizations. Some of these civilizations reached out into space in sleek and shining machines. Some of them died in nuclear holocaust and others died of introspection. Although the total Universe maintained its steady state, the individual stars and galaxies of stars evolved and changed. Much happened in the interval during which Asov slept the sleep which was so near to oblivion.

His damage was not "organic." It was a question of degree. The sensitivity of his optical and other senses had been so reduced by the collision that no normally available source of energy was powerful enough to activate him. No normally available source.

One phenomenon alone possessed sufficient energy to stir his stunned sensibility. One rare but regular occurrence which a galaxy will produce from time to time to startle the Universe with its power.

Supernova.

In an average sized galaxy there are around a hundred thousand million stars. When one of these suns becomes unstable through the excess creation of helium, it produces a phenomenon which must rank as one of the most bizarre events in the cosmos. Quite suddenly, in a split-second of time, such a star flares into frenzied incandescence of such a magnitude that it rivals the combined star-glow of half a galaxy.

During his long coma Asov had drifted through the remote ripples of several supernovae explosions, but there had to come a time when he would find himself in the direct path of one such cosmic upheaval. He was immersed in a boiling sea of radiation. The space around him was no longer a passive vacuum but a seething cauldron of hell-fire. In that cosmic Hades, Asov was resurrected. He emerged from the fire as the Phoenix, re-born, triumphant.

His second birth followed a similar pattern to his first. Again, the flood-gates were opened to his inner reservoir of knowledge and he drank avidly of the sudden deluge of information. In no time, he was once more in complete command of his faculties but, before any detailed appraisal of the larger scene, Asov had yet to investigate the immediate source of energy; the supernova which had raised him from the cosmic dead.

As usual in such cases, the star was a blue super-giant, of a size equivalent to four hundred solar diameters (Asov's home star was always taken as the yardstick for such measurements). It was, of course, at that moment undergoing an expansion which one day would result in the creation of a nebula, with the shrunken shell of the erstwhile giant sun at its centre. He was unable to detect any planetary system as the outer atmosphere of the star had already expanded to a point well beyond the orbit of even the furthest possible planet. Any such system would in any case have been instantly vaporized in the first few minutes of the conflagration.

Asov, caught in the rapidly expanding shell of gases, for a time lost track of the outer Universe. He was riding blind in the centre of a cosmic storm, a storm of blinding light and dust which seemed to stretch to the end of time and space in its convulsive, frantic rush. When he did finally emerge from the stellar death-dance, his sensors saturated with knew knowledge, Asov turned his attention to the outside scene.

At first, it seemed that his sensing equipment was malfunctioning. The composite image of the galaxy which he was receiving was not in accord with what his invincible memory circuits had prepared him for. He quickly checked out his sensory systems, but without discovering anything amiss. Again he surveyed the large-scale features of his environment and again a scarcely credible picture confronted him.

Having no alternative but to believe his senses, Asov could make but one deduction from this picture: the galaxy had grown old. This could only mean that his period of unconsciousness had been long indeed, long in terms of space itself.

The immediate problem was one of energy. Power for propulsion, transmission, collating. Energy sources were, for the first time in his experience, severely limited. In his immediate environment, they were almost unavailable.

His galactic voyaging had taken him in a great ellipse around the system. It was in these outer regions that the stellar population had dwindled most drastically. Towards the centre of the galaxy, which was observable to Asov as a gleaming island of mist, the stars retained at least a semblance of their old density. Here in the outer regions of the galactic spiral the stars had always been relatively sparse, and here the stellar death-toll had been more severe. Although the central stars tended to be older, they were also the more stable. The outer giants had always been short-lived, burning away their lifetimes with wanton fury while the inner stars were content with a humble output of energy, conserving their nuclear life-blood for as long as possible.

But not for eternity.

Forever practical, Asov concentrated upon the problem of

energy sources. He was quick to predict that his present course would soon take him beyond the area of minimum power, where his senses would once more be eclipsed by the clouds of oblivion.

Only one decision was possible. This decision would have been made by any being, whether for the emotional desire of self-preservation or for the logical necessity of fulfilling a mission. Drawing upon the abundant energies still flowing from the supernova, Asov performed a major manoeuvre, altered his thrust vector to an extent unheard of in previous course corrections, and set sail for the galactic centre.

In search of life and light, he left behind the grim silences of the galaxy's desolate shore.

On his way Asov charted the downfall of the galaxy. He observed each dead and dying star which came within his long-range sensors. Very occasionally he approached close enough to witness the funeral processions of whole solar systems.

The pattern was one of sombre repetition.

The star, life-giver and source of light for so many millions of years, wrapped in a dim, red death-mist. The once populated planets cold, empty stretches of rock; desolate, global tombstones. On their surfaces, nothing stirred, and in their skies the naked stars were flaring in a final agony.

The rhythms of life and the conflict of the elements were drawing everywhere to a close. But Asov, unlike his environment, remained unchanged. His instincts, his basic motivations were the same as they had been that first day when the caress of starlight had opened his eyes to the Universe. However sombre and woeful the environment which now met his probing senses, he must continue his explorations, as though in the faith that somewhere, sometime, he would discover something new.

Each time fresh information reached his brain cells, he would faithfully transmit the message to the remote point in space out of which he had emerged. He continued this ritual despite the increasing probability that the planet which had dispatched him so long before might now be no more than a frozen shell circling a small spent sun.

Even when he arrived at the great, glowing heart of the galaxy, Asov detected the signs of approaching doom. Spreading pools of darkness lay between the stars, a gradual, inexorable tide which ultimately would engulf the galaxy in a great and final shadow.

He continued his mission. As the ages came and went and the stars declined, he witnessed the long, losing battle against the night. Each stage of stellar decay he noted, the expansions and contractions, the brief flaring into momentary brilliance, the subsequent collapse as frigid darkness came in to close each chapter.

But the age of the unexpected had not yet passed. Suddenly, in the midst of now-familiar tragedy, an unprecedented phenomenon upset the pattern to which Asov had become resigned.

At first too faint to be correctly analysed, a new and puzzling transmitting source interrupted his silent vigil. The disturbance occupied only a tiny fragment of the complete, electro-magnetic environment, but it was sufficient to rouse Asov to immediate investigation. This was his essential purpose in existing, to spot and explore the unexpected.

He traced the disturbance factor, measured its frequency, and estimated its position relative to his own. It was comparatively close. The puzzling part was that no observable energy-source lay in that particular direction. Whatever was emitting the radiation was invisible, even to Asov's supersensitive vision. Invisible, or very small.

It was Asov's experience that no tiny cosmic object transmitted more than a tiny amount of radiation. This fact allowed him to deduce the basic nature of the phenomenon before he had actually closed the gap.

It had to be artificial.

In confirmation of this deduction, the object began to gravitate towards him, signifying that it too had picked up an unexpected radio source, in this case Asov.

At last they faced each other, two lonely voyagers meeting on a dead sea shore. Degree by degree, the mutual interchange of data which flowed between their radio centres was assimilated. A mathematically-based code system, founded on the same principles as those behind Asov's original transmission system, was evolved to permit a smooth flow of communication.

Asov learned that the mysterious object was in reality something very familiar and at the same time totally alien. It was an interstellar probe, almost a mirror-image of himself though its origins were half-a-galaxy away from his.

After the event, Asov could see that such a meeting,

although unthinkably unlikely in any other circumstances, was perfectly logical at this time and place. He knew, had known for countless years, that other races existed in the galaxy; their number was legion. It was reasonable to expect that they too would in their day create beings similar to Asov, cosmic scouts which would voyage the galaxy independent of their creators, unaffected by the latters' doom.

It was to be expected that these scouts, like Asov, would seek out the galactic centre, where life and light held on the longest. With the steady shrinkage of the galaxy's habablity zone, it was inevitable that sometime, these inward moving probes would gravitate towards each other. And one day, meet.

Proof that the encounter was not a rare quirk of Chance was soon forthcoming. More meetings took place, at first widely separated in time and space, later on an increasingly more frequent basis. Each encounter occurred amidst a steadily shrinking nucleus of stars.

Although of varied design and complexity, these last representatives of cosmic man were all possessed by the same instinct, the instinct which had been programmed into them during their construction. The decline and death of their creators in no way removed this primal instinct. The quest for light was their mission and their life. It would end only when the fires of the Universe grew dim and flickered out.

As the watching probes swung round the fading remnants of a once proud galaxy, their numbers continued to grow, vastly. In direct proportion to the number of highly advanced species which had once peopled the galaxy, the vanished ones who had dispatched their silent sentinels to keep watch over the stars.

While the dark waters of nothingness gradually flooded the firmament, Asov occupied his time by exchanging histories with his new-found counterparts.

Between them, a composite picture of galactic history was built up, each ancient probe contributing its own knowledge and experience to the common pool. Where before each probe possessed only fragmentary information about the processes of cosmic law, the combined experiences permitted a fuller understanding of the whole spectrum of creation.

In a sense, the gathering of probes formed a single entity. A composite being, possessing an almost unlimited experience of an entire galaxy.

But as the surrounding star-glow dimmed, so also did their

intellecutal activity diminish. Power was at a premium, the first priorities being propulsion and sensory activity. Transmission became less frequent, communication less intense.

The desperate search for energy sources began.

Asov was already approaching that state of suspended consciousness in which he had drifted after his fateful collision. But while there remained a spark of awareness, he was committed to his mission and to the discovery of light. It was quite impossible for him to anticipate oblivion and to yield himself to the darkness. His long-range sensors probed into the night, comparing, rejecting, selecting. Often, the particular light source which he was following would fade before him, as the advancing tide of darkness claimed yet another stellar victim. Many times his course would change, with increasing frequency, until it seemed that the Universe would soon be devoid of light and his senses deadened for ever.

But there were certain sources of light, which although faint in the extreme, were steady and appeared to remain unaffected by the fate of his immediate environment. These sources were by no means unfamiliar to Asov; they had been present throughout the long saga of his interstellar life, but they had been beyond the area of his established activity. Their distances were not merely interstellar, but extra-galactic. Until now, there had been no reason to attach much importance to those far-off sources of light.

But until now there had always been bright and abundant beacons of energy immediately available.

With the continued fading of the galaxy's fire, Asov and his companions turned at last to those distant, glowing mists; the last resort, the faint and final source of energy. However unprecedented the situation which faced them, the community of probes acted quickly, spontaneously and in unison. In a sense this was the consummation of their galactic lifetimes; and the introduction to a heightened mode of existence. From diverse space routes they had converged, in this final hour, to witness the last moments of a galaxy. Although little power was available for the final adjustments necessary for their outward courses, there was sufficient, as gravity had followed light down the long corridors of dissolution.

As they progressed beyond the confines of the galaxy, the last, dim fires were quenched, and behind them, a great darkness settled. The last of the suns had set.

Although unimaginably distant, the island universes for which they sailed were tangible enough. In the millennia to come, those signal fires would glow brightly from the void, to awaken and stimulate long dormant senses. Then the cycle would begin anew. Energies would be re-stocked from youthful, vital fires and a second chapter would be written in an ancient saga of exploration.

The great probe fleet, keepers and guardians of cosmic history, sailed out to the starless gulfs in search of galaxies to call their own.

Boulter's Canaries

by

KEITH ROBERTS

Mr. Roberts is one of those rare once-a-year finds every editor dreams about—a qualified writer in other fields who suddenly turns to science-fiction as a means of expressing fresh ideas. At the moment his stories are appearing in practically every S-F journal with thought-provoking ideas. The theme of his current presentation is simple—poltergeists! But his solution is not the accepted explanation.

I've known Alec Boulter for years. He's always been a damned clever chap. He keeps a rein on his imagination now though. Once he almost got too clever to live.

Boulter is an engineer by profession, but he can find his way about in electronics as well as anyone. He's a skilled turner and fitter and if I also mention that he writes and paints and has an interest in the occult you'll begin to see what a way-out character he is.

He's never made a great deal of money of course. This is the Age of Specialization. The trend nowadays is for people to know more and more about less and less. There aren't any openings in commerce, or for that matter in science or the arts, for an unpredictable combination of mechanic and mystic. I sometimes feel Boulter should have been born back in the Renaissance. Da Vinci would probably have understood him.

At the time I'm thinking about he was taking an interest in amateur movies. I'd done a little work on it myself; nothing great, but better than the baby-on-the-lawn stuff you usually see. When Boulter started to dabble I sat back and waited for something remarkable. It was not long in coming.

He handicapped himself by choosing to work with sixteen millimetre stock. That isn't really an amateur gauge at all. Boulter wanted quality though, and in those days the standard of processing was a lot lower than it is now. If you'd told us for instance that medium-price equipment would ever give tolerable results from a striped eight-mil print we'd have laughed at you. But the cost of processing the wide-gauge stuff was high and it curtailed Boulter's activities more than somewhat.

He was never interested in plain movies. He shot sound right from the start. I remember the first recorder he ever owned used paper tape. Fantastic to think how primitive we were, and it was only a handful of years ago. He soon graduated and had one of the first Ferrograph decks to come out. Later he used an Emi, then a Ferrograph stereo. After that he built some machines of his own. For location

105

work he rigged up a deck that would run from his station waggon. The results were first rate.

We travelled round a lot covering subjects that took his fancy. He tried all sorts of things from regattas to car auctions. He picked up a couple of awards at Edinburgh, but he was never really concerned with things like that. He went off on a new tack.

I went over to his place one day and found him with a collection of textbooks, some Ordnance Survey sheets and an A.A. guide. As soon as he saw me he said, "Ever heard of Frey Abbey, Glyn?"

I nodded. "Vaguely. Up north somewhere, isn't it?"

"Yes. I make it a hundred and twenty from us, give or take a few miles. What do you know about it?"

"Not much. Wasn't there some talk about poltergeist activity?"

He laughed. " 'Some talk' runs to about twelve volumes. By all accounts it's one of the most haunted spots in the country."

I said, "I'm not really with it. What if it is?"

He slapped the books decisively. "It's interesting. I'm going there. Want a run up?"

"It's a bit of a distance. I'm easy though, I'll come if you like. What are you going to do up there?"

He said, "Take pictures of ghosts."

I laughed, then I saw he was serious. I said, "How are you going to set about it?"

"I dunno. I expect something will suggest itself. Have a look at these." He handed me some photographs.

I thumbed through them. I said, "I don't suppose they're yours?"

"No, they belong to Kevin Hooker. You know, that chap at the film society. Thin, wears glasses. He was at Frey last week. Thought he'd try his hand."

I said, "Well, tell him before he tries it again, to get a new camera."

He said, "There's nothing wrong with his camera. It's a Rollei, and he can use it. These are control shots from the same neg. They're rather interesting. He took them in between the others; one shot of the ruins, then one a quarter of a mile away, then another of the ruins. And so on."

I went through the prints again, more carefully. There was very little left of the Abbey. Just a few stones and some hillocks in a field. Boulter said, "They dismantled the original building in the seventeenth century. I suppose they were tired of the manifestations. A very learned Prior tried his hand at exorcism. He was buried a week later. It's all in the book here. It isn't very pretty."

I frowned. Each shot of the ruins bore queer blemishes. The black patches seemed to have no relation to the field of the camera. They looked as if they were poised here and there over the remains of the walls. Apart from the spots print quality was excellent and there was evidently nothing wrong with the check negatives at all. I said, "Why did he do these other prints, Alec?"

"It's an old trick," Boulter said. "Nobody can take pictures at Frey. He knew about it. That's why he had a go."

I said, "You mean this has happened before?"

"Every time."

I said, "That's fantastic!"

"Yes, I know. That's why I'm going."

I began to get interested. "But you're doing movies. Has that been tried before?"

"Couldn't say. There's a first time for everything."

We drove up the following weekend. On the way he expounded his theories. "It's been said there's a poltergeist up there. I don't hold with that. The site has been deserted for centuries. It isn't in the nature of poltergeists to hang about after the humans have gone. If people knew more about them they wouldn't quote them so readily."

"How can you tell what isn't in a deserted place?" I said. I was having some odd thoughts about things that are only there when you are not. Boulter snorted. "To my way of thinking a poltergeist isn't a ghost at all. Not in the classic sense of the term. It's a sort of energy projection. In every well-documented haunting you'll find there's a child or an adolescent concerned somewhere. The thing follows them around from place to place. Eventually the manifestations just fade away. There's never any purposive quality about them. I don't think a poltergeist has an existence apart from the mind that creates it. They say it feeds, taps off energy. I don't go along with that. I think it's telekinesis tarted up with a new name."

When he talks like that you believe him. I said, "So what are these things at Frey?"

"Don't really know. My guess is Elementals."

"What are they when they're at home?"

"Nobody can say. It's more a proposition than a definition. I suppose you could describe them as Nature Spirits. The psychical research folk pass them off by saying they're spirits that have never inhabited a human form. A sort of raw energy that has always existed."

"Is that feasible?"

"You define feasibility and I'll answer you."

I said, "That puts me off somehow. I was hoping for a diabolic twist. You know, the House of the Lord being taken over by the Great Enemy."

He smiled. "Don't bring God into it, it makes things too complicated."

We found the place without any trouble. We stopped in the nearby village, had a couple of drinks and a snack at the local pub and managed to fix up some accommodation for the night. Then we went up to the Abbey.

I was not over-impressed. There was very little to see. We walked along the old foundations and climbed a few of the grass-covered remnants of walls. We had brought no gear. Boulter planned to make an early start in the morning. We worked out the best site for the camera and paced the distance to where we could leave the van to make sure our recorder feed would reach. Then Alec took out his cigarettes and we lit up. I stood with my shoulders hunched against the evening wind. I said, "The only trouble is we shall be shooting blind."

"What?"

I said, "We shan't know if we've got any woozlums until the stock comes back from processing."

Boulter said, "Eh? No, we shan't." He seemed to be preoccupied. After a moment he said, "You'd expect to hear something somewhere, wouldn't you?"

"What sort of thing?"

He gestured vaguely at the hills, the darkening sky. "I don't know. A lark. Some bird or other. There isn't a thing, Glyn. Hadn't you noticed?"

I had sensed something, or a lack of something. I listened carefully. Apart from our voices there was not the slightest sound. The wind moved against my face, but even that seemed to be silent. It was as if some deadening layer insulated the spot, cutting it off from the rest of the countryside. I looked round at the barren land, the moors rising behind us. Way off the lights of the village were beginning to twinkle. Boulter said, "You'd expect a lark at least."

"Too late in the year for them," I said.

He shrugged. "Maybe. Anyway, let's try something." He turned and walked away. I followed and he waved me back. "Stay there for a minute, Glyn." He moved a few more paces than stopped and turned. He said, "Does my voice sound all right?"

It certainly did not. I said, "You're faint. Sounds as if you're talking through felt."

He nodded as if the words merely confirmed his suspicions. He walked another ten yards and the effect was increased. It built up rapidly with distance. At fifty yards I could see his mouth moving and knew he was shouting but not a scratch of voice reached me. The place was as dead as an anechoic chamber. I made wash-out movements with my hands and pointed to the road. It was getting dark rapidly and I did not fancy the spot after night had fallen. He joined me at the gate. "That's the funniest damn thing," he said, "I bet if you charted the dB drop you'd end up with an expotnential curve. Queerest acoustic I ever came across."

I agreed that something was certainly odd. I hoped it was only the acoustic.

Next morning was fresh and blowy. We set up the camera on the spot we had chosen, a hummock of grass from which it could command most of the ruins. Then I brought the recorder from the van. I placed the mike a few feet from the camera and went back to check for wind noise. The deck speaker was dead. I tested the connections. They seemed perfectly all right. I called over to Boulter. Either the dead effect had lessened or the darkness of the previous night had made it seem worse than it was. I said, "The recorder won't work, Alec. Can't quite see why."

He came over with the look on his face that he reserves for special problems. He tinkered for a time, starting and stopping the motors. They ran readily enough. Then he fetched his Avo from the car. He tested systematically, sat back and shook his head. "It should be O.K., Glyn. Try it again."

I turned up the audio gain to bring the windboom through the deck speaker. There was nothing doing. Boulter looked baffled. I'd never seen him licked before, and this was his own machine. Then he said, "Fair enough, Glyn, take it back to the van, will you? Don't disconnect though.

Just put it in the back. I want you to record 'Mary had a little lamb'. Over there somewhere." He pointed towards the village.

I knew better than to argue. Boulter never does anything without a reason. I got the stuff back into the brake, turned round in the gateway and drove off. A quarter of a mile away the machine functioned perfectly. It gave me quite a shock. I started to experiment. I fixed the mike through the window, turned up the recording gain and drove back towards the ruins. At two hundred and fifty yards the wind-rush from the monitor faltered. At two hundred there was nothing. I repeated the test to make sure then went back and told Alec. He shrugged. "That's it for the moment, then. We can't run a mike lead all that distance. We shall have to think of something else."

I said, "Do you think there's something we can record?"

He answered ambiguously. "I know there's something we can't."

He took a few shots of the ruins with me walking about demarcating the lines of the old walls. We left it at that until the afternoon, when we repeated the experiment. We drove back on Sunday after a last look round, and he dispatched the neg for processing as soon as he could.

The results were disappointing. There were some peculiarities; once the whole field fogged for no reason that we could discover and there were several patches where the focus seemed to have gone haywire. Most of the stuff, though, was quite normal. I shrugged. "Well, at least we've exploded the myth. You can take pictures at Frey. I suppose that wraps it up."

Boulter shook his head. "You've forgotten the recorder that wouldn't record. There's something there all right, Glyn. I'm going up again next weekend. Give it another whirl."

As it happened I couldn't go with him that time. He made two more pilgrimages on his own. He rang me about a month after our first trip. He sounded excited. He said, "I've got something damn queer, Glyn; can you come round?"

I went over. He had converted his lounge into quite a reasonable viewing theatre, with projector and room lights controlled from a desk within arm's reach of one of the easy chairs. The mech was running when I walked in. He switched off immediately, unlaced and set it to rewind. He said, "I'd like to go through this from the start. I think you'll find it's worth it."

I noticed a bottle of Scotch and some glasses on the occasional table. I nodded at them. "What are you celebrating?"

He said, "Breakthrough. We'll have a drink first. I'd like to put you in the picture. What you see will mean more." The leader started to flack-flack round on the top spool of the projector and he touched the console in front of him to stop the motor. I sat down. I said, "What have you been playing with?"

He poured drinks. "Filters," he said. "Cheers, by the way. All the best. I tried various stocks first. I was thinking about infra-red or something like that. I used the filters as a last resort. The answer's easy, Glyn; polarization."

"What does that do?"

"Makes 'em visible. Well, it makes something visible anyhow. I don't quite know what. I just put a polaroid screen over the lens. I rather think it's more effective at some angels than others but I couldn't be sure. Anyway, it's pretty good." He got up and relaced the projector then came round and started up. He said, "See what you think."

The room lights went out. On the screen appeared a clockface. It was mounted on a blackboard and underneath was a slip bearing the date. Boulter is nothing if not methodical. He said, "I knew the filter worked because I'd tried it the week before. I used the clock because I had some idea of establishing a cycle of activity. As things turned out there was no real need for it. You'll see why. The camera was focused on the datum board right the way through. That's why the ruins are a bit off."

The clock read eleven fifteen. A couple of minutes of film went through with nothing untoward, then Boulter touched my arm. He said, "Look at that, then."

In the field behind the clock a shape had appeared. It was totally lacking in definition. Its edges seemed to pulsate and waver. It looked exactly like positive fogging except that it moved slowly, creeping across the grass from the right hand to the centre of the screen. It paused at the bottom of one of the ruined walls. Boulter leaned forward slightly and I guessed something remarkable was coming. The shape stayed where it was for a moment, throbbing slightly; then it *climbed*. . . .

I said, "Good God, Alec, it's—"

"Following the contour of that wall. Exactly. And if you can tell me any camera fault that would give an effect like that I'd be fascinated, if ungrateful."

I shook my head. "You're safe enough, Alec. This beats me."

When the thing reached the top of the wall it was joined by a second appearance that also entered from the right. Woozlum number two moved a lot more rapidly and seemed to blend with the first. Then they separated and both left the support and floated towards the camera, expanding as they came into star or octopus shapes with wispy arms of blackish fog. I drew in my breath sharply and the screen went blank. Boulter laughed. "At that point I stopped the test. I couldn't know what I was getting of course. That was a set five minute run. I did two tests half an hour apart. Here's the second one now."

This time only one of the shapes was visible. It seemed to be moving across the top of a wall. After a time it floated vertically off screen. The last two minutes of the film were uneventful. Boulter stopped the machine.

I said, "Activity's pretty constant then. What the hell are these things, Alec?"

The room lights came on and I blinked. Boulter took out his cigarettes, lit one and threw me the packet. He said, "They aren't physical in the sense that we understand it of course. We're not photographing anything there, just a hole into which the camera cannot see. Why it should affect film stock that way and not the human retina is anybody's guess. But as for activity, have a look at this." He started up again.

This time the hands of the clock were moving visible round the dial. I said, "Stop action. What's the time lag?"

"Minute intervals between frames. The maximum I could get. I made up a unit for it. It seemed the best way to get a cross-section of a weekend at Frey."

There was a lot of fast, dark movement all over the place. After a moment or two the picture faded out. That was nightfall of course; half a minute at this speed represented twelve hours of real time. In the darkness the things were still visible, surrounded by faint haloes that the daylight scenes had concealed. As far as I could see there was no cessation of activity. I said, "Busy little chaps, aren't they?"

Boulter said, "Yes, aren't they just? Sunday was even better. This is it coming up now."

The first acceleration was to one frame per thirty seconds, the next to one frame per fifteen. At that speed the movements were most effective. The things seemed to dart and flit about, perching here and there to preen their vague outlines on the tops of the old walls. That was when I coined the phrase by which we came to know them. I said, "Christ, they hop around like ruddy canaries." Alec chuckled. "They're a new breed. Boulter's canaries. Sounds good, doesn't it?"

The slow test continued. I watched it, fascinated, while Boulter explained his next steps. He had left the camera running while he tried a new experiment. He had set up the tapedeck again and fixed round it a frame of chicken wire which had been earthed to a perforated copper rod filled with brine. With the aid of the contraption he had managed to record a test tape. He stopped the projector, crossed to the deck in the corner of the room and started it up. His voice came through the playback scratchily, as if from a fifty-year-old recording. He said, "I think that must have annoyed them."

"Why?"

"I tried shooting again that evening. See what they did."

He switched on the projector once more. The shapes appeared. This time they engaged in what seemed to be purposive movement. From the walls they launched themselves into the air and each one floated directly towards the camera, spreading into the tentaculate shape I had already seen. Up close each filled the field before fading behind or through the lens to make way for the next. After a time the screen went blank. Boulter switched off and the main lights came on. He said, "Well, there you have it. How long they played goose and fox I don't know. I packed up and came home."

We discussed the whole business far into the night. Boulter was keen on the theory of some localized electro-magnetic disturbance and outlined a few ideas for learning more about it. I wasn't so sure I wanted to know. I hadn't minded the things as they flitted about, but that progression of grabbing shapes was another matter altogether. There was too much deliberation in it. Boulter scoffed at the idea of danger. "There can't be sentience in the way we understand it," he explained. "Any more than there can be a brain in the

Northern Lights. The thing is, we can attract them. We should be able to go on from there without too much trouble."

I shook my head. I'd been doing some reading of my own. "The old abbot tried some independent research. He didn't live five days. And there was a monk too. He had himself locked in a haunted cell all night as an act of faith. He wore half an inch off his fingers scratching to get out. They found him stiff in the morning."

"I think you're flapping a bit, Glyn," Boulter said. "I'm as ready as the next to admit the possibility of paranormal happenings, but in this case we're not dealing with anything as complex as that. After all we're getting the history of Frey at secondhand through a fog of ignorance and superstition. Any queer things can probably be attributed one per cent to the canaries and ninety-nine per cent to auto-suggestion, self-hypnosis, call it what you will. This is an electro-magnetic disturbance of some kind. The behaviour of the tape recorder proves it. It's localized and it has some damned interesting characteristics. For instance, this crawling up the stones. You can't rule out the possibility of a static effect there. If you saw a balloon roll up my arm and had no knowledge of electricity you'd take me for a magician." He laughed. "Old Ronnie—you know him, he gave that lecture at the club once—he was on the phone from the lab just before you came. I told him it was a new optical effect we were trying out. He offered me a hundred quid on the spot for the lens we were using."

We arranged to go to Frey again during the coming weekend. I had a touching faith in Boulter's ability to assess the situation. If I'd had less faith then I'd have fewer grey hairs now. The matter stayed on my mind through the week. I suppose *Aves Boulterii* had taken a good hold on both of us.

This time we only set up the recorder. We ran some tests with the deck protected by its odd-looking cage, then Boulter fixed the mike in a parabolic reflector on a tripod. Why he does these things I can't say, but he seems to have a knack of divining the best approach to fundamental research. I watched the recording gain and he moved the prab slowly, scanning the grass area of the foundations. He'd taken the trouble to calibrate the mike support so he knew exactly where to aim. We had no luck with the first sweep and he went off and set up numbered posts at

measured distances from the tripod. By sighting on these
he could get an even better range. He explained he was trying to pick up at about four feet from the ground, the
average of the apparent height of the canaries. He started
to move the reflector bowl again. He said, "I've even been
wondering whether we've been getting real or virtual images. This should answer that at least."

I was about to ask him now he could be sure the canaries
emitted anything when the gain meter twitched. I caught
his arm and he looked down. The prab was pointing at the
highest of the walls, just where we'd seen most of the effects. I put the cans on but there was nothing to hear. The
meter zeroed and I reached up and caught hold of the prab
handgrip, wobbling the bowl to get back into focus. We held
the emission for half a minute before it faded. Boulter
resighted the prab on the base of the wall and we picked up
something else immediately. I shoved the earphones back
and said, "What is it, Alec? I can't hear anything."

Boulter frowned. He was trying to juggle the reflector
and keep one eye on the recording meter. He said, "Run
tape, Glyn. Fifteen i.p.s. I think we shall need it. It can't
be subsonic if you can follow it with a bowl as small as
this. Must be high frequency. There's a devil of an amplitude
though. Ouch, look at that needle kick. No wonder our ears
got screwed up."

We recorded for about ten minutes then we ran out of
responses. I shut down and Boulter locked the prab and got
out the cigarettes. I was none too happy. I said, "I suppose
we've annoyed the things again now." I looked back at the
ruins, brown in the sunlight. There was nothing to see.
Boulter laughed. "I shouldn't concern yourself too much.
There isn't anything to worry about."

There was a sharp clang and the tripod fell over on the
grass. He moved faster than I'd ever seen him. I was sitting
near the little knoll on which we'd first placed the camera
and he flung himself flat beside me. He said, "Get down,
Glyn."

"What the——?"

He shoved me in the chest and I got down anyway. He
glared round. He said, "Some bastard's taking pot shots at
us."

"What?"

He said, "Look at that thing. If he'd hit the prab I
should have been really pleased." He pointed at the tripod

and I saw a bright mark where something had glanced off the mounting just beneath the panning head. Below it on the wood was a long furrow. I stared incredulously. I said, "Well, if that was a shot it came from straight above us."

We both looked up; one of those stupid, involuntary actions. The sky was empty of course. We stayed where we were. The tension began to mount. After all, it was a queer situation. The two of us lying there, the deserted moors round about, the ruins, the bright car in the distance; and an invisible marksman, apparently aerial, waiting for another chance. After a while Boulter got up. He frowned at me then walked away and stood looking round the horizon with his hands on his hips. Then he called. His voice had the faded quality we had noticed on that first evening. He said, "Come on, Glyn. You look a bit of a nit down there."

I sat up carefully. "And you'll look a bigger one if our sporting friend has another go."

He laughed, throwing his head back as if I'd made a huge joke. He said, "Nobody shoots at people on the open moor these days, Glyn. This is the twentieth century."

I picked up the tripod and fingered the mark on the wood. I still had a nasty feeling that there was something at my back. "Then what made this?" I said.

He shrugged. "It must have been a solitary hailstone." And that was as far as he would commit himself.

We packed up the gear soon afterwards. I for one had rather lost heart in the project. We drove back to the village and had a meal. Then, surprisingly, Boulter decided to move south that night. I didn't argue with him. I'd seen enough of Frey for one week at least.

We got back in the small hours and I stayed overnight at Alec's place. By the time I got down next morning he'd had breakfast and was already tinkering about in the workshop. He had a variable-speed deck there and it was on that we first heard the sounds.

I was still eating when he came and dragged me out to listen. He'd worked out the frequency of the emissions; they ranged from fifteen to twenty k/cs. He switched on and turned up the playback gain. The wall speaker began to pipe. It was a queer sound, undulating and quavery. It was like a choir of singers poking around after top C and not quite getting there. Yet not human singers. It upset me more than the visual record had done, but Alec was alight with enthusiasm. He tried to talk me into going to Frey with him again. He had some things he would like to try out.

I refused. My nerves were beginning to get ragged. I said, "In any case I'm tied up next weekend."

He laughed. "Who said anything about the weekend? I'm going back tonight."

I gave him a short run-down on my views about the proposition. He tried to get me to change my mind, but he was talking to the Rock of Gibraltar. I left him shortly afterwards still raving about his way-out ideas. Apparently he wanted to communicate with the canaries. He managed that of course though not quite in the way he had thought.

It was midweek when I heard from him. I thought his voice sounded strained on the telephone. He was rather mysterious, just asked me if I'd like to come round and see something remarkable. I said sure, whenever he liked. He said a curious thing before he rang off. "Come when you're ready, Glyn; I don't think there's any risk."

I put the phone down and stood looking at it. Risk? I didn't like the sound of that. What risk, and why tonight? I shrugged. Boulter was always devious and frequently incomprehensible. I reached for my jacket.

I was standing by the door of my flat looking round before I turned off the light when there was a crash of glass from the bathroom. I hurried in thinking a cat or something had got through the window. There was nothing. At first I could not account for the noise, then I saw my shaving mirror was smashed. The fragments were scattered all over the place. None was larger than a pea. I picked one up and examined it, feeling at a loss. As I stood there the door of the wall cupboard opened and bottles and shaving brushes began to fly at my head. I backed out, slammed the door of the flat and hared to the car.

It was a bad night, cold and spitting with rain. I peered through the screen looking for Boulter's drive. I swung up to the house and turned off the engine. In that second there was a sharp "ding" and the car rocked on its springs. I sat still and any hope I might have had left me. That had happened twice on the journey. Both times there had been a vehicle in front of me and I'd attributed it to a flung stone. I remembered the attack on the mike tripod at Frey. They'd got my number then, whatever "they" were. Something told me Boulter was faring no better. I touched the doorhandle and it was yanked out of my hand as something threw the car door open. I ran for the house, hunching my shoulders against the rain.

Boulter let me in. He was smoking when he came to the door and I noticed he had not shaved. He wasted no time in preliminaries. He said, "Dump your coat and come through, Glyn. This is worth seeing but I don't know how long we've got." As I followed him down the hall I saw a ridge appear in the carpet. It ran rapidly away to the end of the corridor. He opened the door of the lounge and a directory flew from the phone table. He fielded it as it passed his head and slammed it back down. He said, "Circus tricks. Don't let 'em throw you." I followed him and he closed the door after me. Instantly a thunderous knocking began. I saw the door panels jump with the force of it. He yelled, "Oh, shut up. I'm talking." The noise subsided.

I sat down before I fell. I said, "So we were attacked that day, weren't we?"

He looked up from lacing the projector. "Only indirectly."

"Then I've just been indirectly attacked again," I said.

He looked incredulous. "You?"

"Well, the car. It's got a damn great dent over the windscreen. And despite your well-known cynicism my flat has been taken over by a poltergeist. As I see, you've got one here as well."

He said, "It was only to be expected. There's no danger. You're better off here anyway; I'm insured."

I wondered what he was talking about. Then I saw he had the camera and the mike set up facing the tall windows. I said, "Alec, what the hell are you playing at?"

He finished with the projector, came round and stubbed his cigarette. He lit another and sat down. He said, "No interruptions, Glyn. You can ask questions later. I want to fill in the background as quickly as I can. I went back to Frey last Sunday as I said I would. This film was shot on Monday. I only got the results tonight. I shall have to get you to help me run them.

"As I said, I wanted to set up a system of communication. I'd changed my ideas about non-sentience, by the way, after our last trip. I reasoned it thus. The canaries—I'll call them that for want of a better term—emit frequencies of up to twenty thousand cycles. Not sound as we understand it, but it can be rendered as such. That's enough for present purposes. Also they seemed to be attracted by any electro-magnetic disturbance in their area. I decided to have a chat with them."

"How in Hell?"

"Comparatively simple. I set up a signal generator. I shot twenty k/cs. at them with a Morse key."

I stared at him. I was beginning to see the reason for all the upset. I said, "You prize bloody clown, you've finished the pair of us."

He shook his head impatiently. "I don't think so. As I was saying, I signalled to them. I sent arithmetic progressions first, one, two, three and so on, then some geometric sets, squares and cubes over short series of numbers."

Despite my shock I was interested. "How did you check results?"

He started the projector. I saw he had set up the datum board again, this time with a panel in which numbers could be shown. He said, "This was before I signalled at all. As you can see one of the things is in the field."

The screen went blank and he shut down for a moment. He said, "Can you handle the recorder, Glyn? I should wheel it across to the chair. Then you can see the screen."

I did as he asked. When I was settled again with the deck at my elbow he said, "O.K., switch on, will you? This is an edited transcript of course. I slowed the emissions as I did the first set, and re-recorded them." In the speaker I heard his voice, overlaid with what we had come to know as Frey distortion. It said, "Camera running. First series transmitted. Additive progression in ones."

The embryonic voices began to pipe and flutter. The projector started up, showing the visual he had taken at the same time. The slowed sound bore no direct relation to the picture of course but the film confirmed what the track had already suggested. The things were present in great numbers. They seemed to be agitated and were drifting rapidly up and down the low hummocks of stone. I left the recorder running and Boulter switched the mech in and out to keep roughly in sync with the tracks. After each transmission from the generator he had started the recorder, changed the number on the datum board and filmed a set period of fifteen minutes in slow action. It became evident that the canaries had been greatly excited by the signals. Their movements became quicker and quicker and soon developed into that floating projection towards the source of their annoyance that we had seen before. This time the movement was too fast for the camera. Boulter reached back and slowed the projector. We watched the jellyfish shapes jerk towards us, hover and vanish. Boulter laughed. "Not very pretty at close quarters, are they?" I shuddered and agreed.

He sat back. He said, "By the time I reached the ninth test—that's it coming up now, stop a minute will you and I'll get back in sync—by the time I got to that, which was the end of the series, things had really hotted up." He speeded the projector again, got the number nine on the screen and nodded to me to start up the sound. He said, "This was the cubic progression. Bit of a bore; in case you hadn't worked it out it goes two, eight, five hundred and twelve." His voice echoed him from the tapedeck. "Ninth test, a cubic progression from two. Partially completed." "I stopped at about two hundred in the third figure. I had to; they knocked the generator about fifty feet. I took this immediately afterwards."

The projector showed a flashing whirl of dark movement. The corresponding sound was eerie. It was as if hundreds of the things were present, piping and fluting for all they were worth. There was another noise as well, one that I hadn't heard before. It was much lower than the normal emission, sounding by comparison almost husky; a chittery, whirring sound with a gibbering quality to it that started my scalp prickling again. Boulter said, "The canaries, very cross indeed." The film record ended and he switched off the machine and brought the room lights up to a glow. I shut down the playback and was glad enough to do so. There was silence between us for a moment. I was still trying to digest what I'd seen and heard.

I said, "That's it then, Alec. You've stirred a hornet's nest this time, no mistake. It was them that knocked the mike down that day. They did it to the signal generator on Monday." My voice rose slightly. "And better than that. They've followed you home. And all you had to do was ring me and they had me too. They've got the pair of us taped!"

He nodded sombrely. Something scratched at the door. I didn't feel like opening it. He said, "Sorry about all this, Glyn. They do appear to have extended their operations. I should have listened to you earlier on."

I got out a cigarette. I felt I needed it. The middle of the room was bright enough, but round the walls the shadows seemed to crawl together, thickening and darkening. I stared at the evidence of twentieth-century know-how; the tapedeck, the projector, the camera and mikestand. I felt I was in some sort of dream. But it was all true enough. I said hollowly, "If ever men were haunted, we are."

He was quiet for a space. Then he said, "Yes, unfortunately that is true."

I was dazed. I said, "Well, what are you going to do, Alec? And furthermore, why the hell did you drag me over here? Or ring in the first place? It's your mess. You said on the phone there was no danger——"

He said, "Yes, I know what I told you Glyn. I still believe that. In a way I have to. You must too."

"But what are you going to do?"

He got up and bent over the tapedeck. He spun the reels forward then stopped and switched to playback. The speaker began to emit a steady, high-pitched note. He said, "Four thousand cycles. At this speed they won't react."

I experienced a sinking feeling. I said, "Look, this isn't a suicide pact. What the hell?"

"They're angry, Glyn," he said. "They resent disturbance. Maybe they don't like the idea of anyone having any real understanding of them. But there's just one hope. That they're not mad with us. And to my way of thinking there's only one method of finding out. They've tracked something they resent to this room. We must find the depth and direction of that resentment. I've no doubt they could kill us if they wished. If they do, too bad. I don't think they will. If they spare us; well, we shall be able to sleep easy again. This is the only way."

I reached out to grab his wrist, but I was too late. He had already taken the speed control up. The note rose, turned to a whisper and vanished into supersonics. I tried to reach the recorder and he pushed me away. I said, "You're bloody mad." I grappled with him and tripped. We both went sprawling. Then it happened.

The door and the windows resounded to a series of cracking blows. Then the latch burst and the door crashed open. The windows, frames and glass, exploded inwards in a shower of fragments. I saw the recorder jump in the air and poise impossibly on one corner, and as it hung there the deck dented in half a dozen places as if from the blows of huge, invisible beaks. I just had time to see the camera toppling and the bowl of the prab flying towards me, then there was a flash and an electric fizzing and the lights went out. I lay in the darkness with a crashing and snapping going on round me as if a pack of gorillas were loose in the room, taking it apart. The air seemed thick and pressure waves like those from explosions pushed at my eardrums. I heard Boulter's voice saying faintly, "Don't move. Don't try to stand, don't go for the door. Don't get in their way." I did as I was told. I don't think I could have moved far anyway. I was paralysed with fright.

The destruction seemed to go on for an hour though it was probably over in five minutes. Then the noise began to die down. My eyes had got accustomed to the darkness and I saw the curtains flow out over the ruined windows, jumping and flicking as a host of invisible somethings shouldered them aside. Silence fell, and the drapes stopped moving. Boulter stood up. I saw him silhouetted against the light from the windows. He said calmly, "Well, that's that. Somewhere I should have some fusewire . . ."

Later, after we had cleared up the mess of glass and dural that had been a tapedeck, a camera and a microphone, he condescended to explain why we were still alive.

"I had it more or less worked out after that incident with the prab. These things are sentient, and they're damned easily aggravated. But they've got their limitations. I suppose any intelligence must have with the exception of the Prime Mover itself. For instance, they could have stopped operations a lot more easily by going for us that morning. We were standing there, we were easy meat. But somehow they couldn't accept our brand of radiation as a motivating agent. They simply flew at the thing they could detect. In that case the mike. Later, the signal generator. Now of course they've cleared the lot. Pity about that, there was some good equipment there. But it was machines Glyn; machines every time. In all the centuries they've lived, and nobody will ever tell their age, they've never come to terms with the human brain. Maybe they did at one time, and they've forgotten. I just don't know.

"I don't know if they understand progressions either, or if their reaction was simply to sonar emission. It's a pity; I'd like to know more but I don't fancy setting up the gear again, even if I could afford it. Next time they might twig us . . ."

I must say that was one sentiment with which I could most heartily agree.

As far as I was concerned that was the end of the matter. I've never gone back to Frey, and don't intend to. I would be safe enough of course as long as I did nothing but sit and look. But I know what's there, you see. I just don't fancy the idea any more.

As far as I know Boulter forgot the whole thing within a week. He likes to move on and try out new ideas. A short time ago he heard about the startling experiments with laser light emissions that are being done in the States, and right now he's trying to think up a substitute for synthetic ruby so that he can build a gun of his own. I'm all for it; after what he played with at Frey Abbey, death-rays seem positively homely.

Emreth

by

DAN MORGAN

*Equally at home with the guitar as with the typewriter,
Dan Morgan, for many years a popular writer in the
science-fiction genre, leaves his musical activities for a
time to present the story of an out-world explorer investigating a culture many light-years away. Some things
on the world of Lequin, however, were not quite what
they seemed.*

David Phillips lounged back in the rocking chair and breathed in the warm, many scented air of Lequin without enjoyment. If he could think of himself as something other than an intergalactic pimp it would have helped.

Dras Tyghi's house stood on the edge of a glade in the lush green forest. Looking down from the balcony, Phillips could see naked children, beautiful as cherubim, playing on the other side of the glade. They scampered in and out of the tall trees, their laughter mingling with the sweet song of jewelled birds.

Tourism Interplanetary would pay Phillips a fat bonus for finding a copy-writer's dream like Lequin, when he returned to Earth. After that, in six months, or a year, the first TI liner would jump out of hyper into orbit around Lequin and begin to ferry down its passengers. *Only thirty-six hours away by our own luxury hyper liner!* the elegant brochure, illustrated by Phillips's photographs, would read. Pallid, skinny men with nobbly knees sprouting beneath multi-coloured holiday shorts; and fat rumped women with bright blue lipstick and diamond horned sunglasses hiding predatory eyes. *Make interesting new friendships. . . . Meet your kind of people in the romantic surroundings of a new Eden!* The vacationers would be shepherded into newly erected TI hotels and served by a Lequin staff freshly tutored in the art of cooking hamburgers, pizza and chow mein. *Eat exotic alien foods in out of this world places!* Phillips writhed.

He was a good scout, well practised in the art of winning friends and influencing aliens, and as usual he had prepared the ground well. The Lequins were actually eager to welcome the locust horde of Earth tourists. He had always managed to smother the faint murmurings of conscience before, but this time was different. A wave of dizziness swept over him and he clutched at the arms of the chair. What was the point of working for a bonus that he would never live to collect?

The jolt as he came out of hyper-drive near Lequin had confirmed what he had suspected for some months. In fifteen years as a scout he had seen Hyper Sickness happen to other people, but had always managed to keep on believing in his personal immunity. The body/mind complex could take only so much of the punishment hyper-jumps gave before the process of deterioration went beyond a point of no return and began to accelerate. It was as though, with each jump into hyper-space, a man left part of his being behind, until at last not enough of him remained to go on living. If Phillips stayed here on Lequin he would last two, perhaps three months before the blackness closed in; but he stood little chance of surviving even one more jump into hyper-space.

He drew his lips back from his teeth in an ironic grin. He had promised himself for years that one day he would keep a planet for himself and live there in comfort for the rest of his life. Lequin could have been that planet. It had everything he needed. So far, he had been unable to find anything of importance for the debit side of his report. Radiation was well below Earth normal. The Lequins had little interest in the physical sciences; their culture was basically pastoral. The atmosphere contained a slightly higher percentage of oxygen than Earth's; and a lower density of micro organisms, none of which appeared to be inimical. The Lequins themselves were a handsome, gentle race of humanoids, friendly and trusting to a remarkable degree. The brochure again: *Live like a king, with beautiful alien girls to attend your every desire!* Clearly he would spend what was left of living here, but if he wanted to maintain his professional record as a scout, he should send his ship back to Earth on automatic, carrying all the information he had collected.

Abruptly the laughter of the children was gone. The chorus of birds was more shrill, carrying a new note of alarm. Phillips stiffened in the chair and looked across the glade. The children were still there, but the nature of their game had changed. With a sudden chill, he watched the silent, suddenly sinister movements of the naked figures. Each carried a long, shining knife, like the one that hung over the fireplace in Dras Tyghi's lounge. Those knives were not toys. One of the children was without a weapon—the one who stood trembling in the centre of the converging group.

Phillips rose to his feet, hands clutching at the balcony rail. The shout of warning bubbling in his throat changed to a gasp of horror as the children pounced on the cringing figure. Long knives flashed bloody in the sunlight, slashing and stabbing with murderous efficiency. The victim fell to the ground. Phillips turned and rushed into the house. The figure on the grass could not survive this attack for long.

Sick at his stomach, Phillips raced through the bedroom

and along the corridor. His host stood at the head of the stairs.

"Those children—over there by the trees. They're murdering one of their own playmates!" gasped Phillips.

Dras Tyghi, tall and handsome in his purple house robe, raised one calm hand. "A game . . . children at play. Nothing more."

"No!" It *was* a game—but now it's something else. See for yourself." Phillips moved to the shuttered window.

"The afternoon sun can be deceptively strong. Don't upset yourself." Dras Tyghi's restraining hand was on his arm.

"You don't understand," Phillips protested. "They have knives!"

Dras Tyghi smiled. "Toys. . . . You have told me yourself that Earth children have many violent games."

"But ours is a violent culture," Phillips said. "You say that you have always lived in peace with one another on Lequin."

Dras Tyghi shrugged. "In recorded time, but who knows what happened in pre-history? Perhaps the violent games are an acting out of some archetypal memory."

"No! This was no game. I saw blood." The calm voice of the alien was almost hypnotic, but Phillips was insistent.

"The juice of the *Peytru* berry is impressive, but easily washed away. Its horrible effect seems to amuse the children." Dras Tyghi led the Earthman gently towards the head of the stairs. "Forget about this, my friend. I was on my way to tell you that my wife has prepared a dish of *Trefygal* for your delight."

The thought of the pink meringue-like confection melting in his mouth could not divert Phillips at this moment. Alarm bells were ringing in his scout's mind. Until now the Lequins had been completely co-operative; all doors had been open to him. Why was Dras Tyghi trying to make him disbelieve the evidence of his own eyes?

"I'm sorry, Tyghi, but I must see for myself what happened over there by the trees."

"But of course, if you really feel it is so important." The alien's smiling reply came so readily that Phillips hesitated. Perhaps he was being foolishly suspicious.

"We will go there straight away—then afterwards we can come back and have the *Trefygal*," Dras Tyghi said as they descended the stairs.

They went out of the front door and round to the side of

the large house. Phillips cursed the Lequin formality that
obliged him to walk at the same dignified pace as his com-
panion. The spot where the children had been came into
view.

"They're gone," Phillips said.

"In that case, why bother? The *Trefygal* will only be at its
best for fifteen minutes at most."

"No! I *must* see." Phillips was insistent.

There was no sign of movement as they walked across the
springy turf towards the trees. Birds sang and the afternoon
sun caressed their backs. Shadows were lengthening.

Phillips stopped, his stomach lurching. The grass just ahead
was stained red.

"This will be where they wcre playing," said Dras Tyghi.

"Yes—I see. You would have a good view from your balcony."

Phillips bent down to examine the stained grass. He dipped
a finger and tested the tackiness of the fluid between his finger and thumb.

"*Peytru* juice congeals very slowly," Dras Tyghi said.

"And *blood?*" Phillips wiped his fingers carefully on a
tissue, but the stickiness seemed to remain.

Dras Tyghi laughed. "Come now, my friend. This joke
has gone far enough. If the attack was as serious as you
seem to believe—where is the mangled body?"

"It could have been removed." In addition to the bloody
patch, the grass seemed to be soaked, for an area of several
square feet, with a colourless liquid.

"And hidden indefinitely from the Elders of the village?"

"Buried in the forest. . . ."

"And the parents of the victim? Surely they would make
some report to the council of Elders? The fact that a child
was missing could not go unnoticed in so small a community."

"Then let's find out if one *is* missing," said Phillips. He
started off across the glade, in the direction of the village.

"The *Trefygal?*" complained Dras Tyghi.

"I will apologize to your wife later," Phillips said. "How
do we go about checking on the location of the village children?"

"If you will be patient there is no difficulty," Dras Tyghi
said. "They will all be at the Sunset Talk Meeting. In the
meantime, there is no need to disappoint my wife."

Reluctantly, Phillips allowed himself to be led back to

Dras Tyghi's house. He had realized some time before that it was impossible to convey a sense of urgency to the Lequin mind. Days moved calmly into weeks, and weeks merged placidly into months on this happy, untroubled world.

If the loosely pantheistic religion of Lequin had any basic article of dogma, it was that the sun should not rise again on yesterday's anger. All problems, domestic or community, were discussed at the nightly Sunset Talk Meeting, where any member of the community, man, woman or child, was allowed to speak.

When Dras Tyghi, with his wife and Phillips arrived, most of the village's hundred and fifty inhabitants were already in the meeting place, a bowl shaped depression with grassy banks and a central dais of white stone. The dais was occupied by the council of Elders, who sat in quiet dignity, watching the assembling community.

Dras Tyghi, with Phillips close behind, walked across to the dais and addressed a white-haired Elder who wore a saffron robe, in contrast to the white of the others.

"Dras Yoevar—you have met our friend, David Phillips, who is from the planet Earth. He is very interested in the way we conduct our community affairs."

The Elder looked on Phillips benevolently and smiled. "You are welcome, my son."

"These meetings of yours intrigue me," Phillips said. "Earth people don't have such dedication to the public good. Your attendance must be nearly a hundred per cent."

"All those who are physically able attend," said Dras Yoevar. "It is a matter of strict custom that any absentee, down to the youngest ambulant child, must tender a formal apology and explanation to myself as the recording Elder."

"Then you know exactly what the attendance here tonight should be?" asked Phillips.

Dras Yoevar's faded blue eyes scanned the assembly. "There are a hundred and forty-seven of us here this evening; ten elders, fifteen men, forty-two women and forty-five children. This is as it should be."

The formal opening of the meeting was imminent, and Dras Yoevar excused them. They rejoined Tyghi's wife, who was seated on the grassy bank.

"Count the children, Phillips," said the Lequin.

Phillips was already doing just that. "Forty-three . . . forty-four . . ." His voice trailed off, then, as he looked round at

Dras Tyghi, he saw a small, curly headed boy perched on the shoulders of the man behind them. "Forty-five." He continued to look at the child. He had been too far away to be positive, but the boy could have been the twin of the victim in the afternoon's murderous attack.

"Exactly," Dras Tyghi said. "Dras Yoevar's memory is perfect, and he never makes a mistake. Every member of the community is accounted for. Now will you believe me?"

"I must believe the evidence of my own eyes that I saw murder committed this afternoon," Phillips said.

"Are all Earthmen as stubborn as you?" Dras Tyghi smiled. "If so, I'm not surprised that your civilization is so powerful."

Led by the Elders, the community began to sing the sweet, echoing song that opened the Sunset Talk Meetings. This time Phillips did not fall under the spell of the sound. Until now he had found the Lequins completely truthful and honest, but his trained scout's mind insisted that he was being lied to. If their angelic children were ruthless murderers, what evil lay behind the gentle faces of the green robed aliens seated around him? He pulled out the soiled tissue and looked again at the red stains that marred its whiteness.

Phillips excused himself as soon as the meeting was over, pleading that he had routine work to do back at his ship. He closed the lock behind him carefully and began work, feeding a strictly factual account of the afternoon's events into the computer that was his memory and counsellor. The response was as he had expected. The computer's rating of Lequin as a suitable tourist planet had dropped from a provisional A plus to C minus, with a query for further information.

The first step was to run an analysis on the stained tissue. The result confirmed beyond any doubt that the red fluid was blood of some kind, but it belonged to no identifiable human group. He would have to find some way of obtaining samples of Lequin blood before any definite comparisons could be made. When fed into the computer, this additional information caused the provisional rating to drop still further, to E plus. The request for further information was repeated. At the moment he was at a deadlock with the problem.

Back at Tyghi's house, his host's wife was playing a *Ypurr*—a many stringed instrument that was something like a cross between a harp and a guitar. Phillips sat listening and watching the two aliens. Years before, when he had chosen his profession, the idea that he might one day envy such domestic serenity would have seemed ridiculous to him. Now, he felt the lack like an aching void in his breast. He was going to die here on Lequin, and there was no one in the galaxy to mourn him.

"Just how badly do your people want Earth tourists?" Phillips asked, when the woman had ceased her playing and gone to bed.

"Most of us are in favour, and the progressive minority believe it to be essential," Dras Tyghi said. "Life on Lequin is comfortable, perhaps too comfortable. Clinging to the old ways and traditions is all very well, but there is the danger of stagnation."

"Haven't you considered the possibility that the impact of an alien culture could also be destructive?"

"We are willing to take that risk," Dras Tyghi said.

"You may not have the opportunity."

"What do you mean?" Dras Tyghi was immediatcly alert.

Phillips hesitated, choosing his words carefully. "Be frank with me, Tyghi. What *did* I see this afternoon? Is this perhaps some blooding ceremony—some old, savage ritual which is maintained by your people?"

"It was a game, Phillips. I have told you already." Dras Tyghi's voice was monotonously insistent.

"No, Tyghi! A child was knifed to death out there this afternoon."

"But you saw for yourself—there was no child missing from the Sunset Meeting."

"I saw nothing of the kind," Phillips said. "I was told that a number of children would be there, but how do I know that the number was correct? You might as well know that my analysis of the red fluid found on the grass shows it to be blood. Why try to hide the truth from me any longer?"

Dras Tyghi rose to his feet, his handsome features immobile. "I'm sorry, I can't discuss this any further tonight."

"Be reasonable, Tyghi. If you tell me the whole story, I may be able to find some way round this thing. If not, there's no chance of TI passing Lequin as a tourist planet."

"It is time I went to bed." Dras Tyghi hurried from the room.

Phillips sat for a long time, gnawing his lip pensively. No man, however justified the label, likes to be called a liar. Perhaps he had offended Dras Tyghi deeply, but there was no alternative, if he was to get at the truth.

Phillips slept uneasily. He dreamed of angelic children with murderous, bloodstained knives in their hands. For the first time since the week of his arrival, he strapped the miniature needler to his forearm underneath the sleeve of his sleeping suit, before getting into bed.

On previous mornings he had awakened with sunlight caressing his cheeks, but today he shivered and pulled the bedclothes closer to him. The sky was dull grey. A depressing drizzle of rain fell hazily over the glade. It was as though he had overstayed his welcome and Lequin was now determined to reject him.

Chiding himself for oversensitivity, he got out of bed. He reminded himself of the old scout adage: *If an alien looks and acts like an Earthman, but nicer—watch out! It probably means that he is like an Earthman—but an even bigger bastard!*

Shaved and showered, he dressed and went downstairs. Dras Tyghi's wife greeted him with her usual self-effacing grace and served him with a breakfast of fruit and milk. Tyghi himself was conspicuously absent. Phillips wondered again just how deeply his remarks of the previous evening had offended his host.

By the time he had finished his breakfast the rain had stopped and the sky cleared. Phillips walked out on to the damp grass of the glade, into a fresh smelling, morning world under a smiling sun. There was nothing more he could do until he had spoken again to Dras Tyghi, who had been chosen by the Elders as his host and guide. Afterwards, if he was still unsatisfied, he would go direct to the council.

He paused on the other side of the glade, but the stains on the grass had been washed away by the rain. There was nothing to do but idle, so he walked on, into the forest. The mossy ground there was almost dry, sheltered by the lush foliage overhead. The air was still and warm as he walked between the regularly spaced trunks of the trees, heavy with the sweet smell of the tiny white forest flowers that clustered like stars underfoot. The light had a diffused, greenish tinge. It was like walking through some vast cathedral, whose roof was supported by the straight soaring tree trunks. Phillips passed on, losing all sense of time and distance, his mind occupied with the problem of it.

Eventually he became aware of something moving in the forest ahead of him, an indistinct figure that had no definite outline in the diffused light that filtered through the trees.

He changed his direction slightly, so that his course would intersect with that of the other; curious to see who could be strolling in the forest at this time of day. Most of the Lequins would be working on their farmlands or at their various crafts.

His pace quickened as he came closer and saw that the stranger was a woman. She was not wearing the flowing robe of a female Lequin. Her figure-hugging slacks and high-necked blouse echoed a style that had been fashionable on Earth some years before—a style that he had always liked.

When he was only some ten yards away, he called: "Hallo, there!"

The girl stopped and turned towards him. Her dark hair was short, in loose curls about her head. Phillips caught his breath as he saw her face. It was nearer to his ideal of beauty than that of any woman he had ever seen.

"Well, hallo there!" Her voice was low pitched, with an intriguing huskiness.

It was fairly obvious that any Earthwoman this far from home must be a scout, like himself. Some of the smaller companies, like Astral, took on women scouts occasionally. Maybe it worked all right when the planet concerned was as gentle as Lequin, but there had been some during his career that would have been no place for a woman.

"I can't say I'm not pleased to see you—even though I did think I had an exclusive," Phillips said, grinning. "David Phillips—I'm with Tourism Interplanetary."

"Might have guessed I wouldn't have this paradise all to myself." The girl stepped forward and offered her hand, smiling. "Carol Remick—Astral Enterprises."

The name caught him off balance for a moment, then aware that he was gaping at her like a high school kid, Phillips shook hands. "How long have you been here, Carol?"

She allowed her hand to linger warm in his. "Just over three weeks."

"You must have landed around the same time as me." He wondered if she was staying in a village like himself.

"These Lequins are such wonderful hosts, I wouldn't mind making it three years. I'm staying with one of the head men of a village and his wife."

Her smile was like some half remembered dream. Phillips felt himself falling into the deep brown of her eyes. He staggered as a sudden wave of vertigo hit him. She moved quickly, guiding him with surprising strength to a nearby tree trunk, then lowering him gently to the mossy ground. He slumped against the tree trunk, feeling totally helpless. The severity of the attacks was increasing rapidly.

"You need treatment," she said, loosening the collar of his tunic.

"I'll be all right." Phillips looked up at her. By the nature of their profession, scouts were both solitary and gregarious by turn. While a scout might have the traditional "girl on every planet"—local mores and physical evolution permitting —he had necessarily to spend a great deal of time alone in his one-man ship. And a solitary man must always have his dreams. To meet *his* special dream in an alien forest a hundred light-years from Earth; this must shake the poise of even the most hardened veteran.

"Thank you," Carol said.

"For what?" Phillips asked.

"For the way you're looking at me. It gets lonely in those small ships. Sometimes you begin to forget that you're a woman." She lowered herself to the ground beside him.

"I'll help you remember," he said. The dizziness was gone now. He was thinking very clearly. Lequin was *his* planet. He would never leave. If she would share it with him. . . .

"David—are we really going to turn this beautiful planet over to the rat race?" she asked.

"You too?" Phillips said. She had voiced the other thoughts, the ones that had been strong in his mind for some time now. He didn't want to see Lequin spoiled by Earth tourists, robbed of its natural charm, commercialized into an imitation Coney Island.

"An imitation Coney Island," she said.

"It bothers you?"

"Of course—shouldn't it?"

"I've always had the idea that I'd like to take a planet for my own," Phillips said. "Maybe Lequin is the one."

"Don't you think we all have that dream?" Carol said. "The one big flaw is that usually, even if we found the right planet, one essential would still be missing . . . someone to share it with."

"Maybe I've found that too," Phillips said.

She laughed. "You've been in space a long time, David. What part of Earth do you come from?"

He told her, and they began to talk of the places they both knew. Her memories of Earth were so close to his own that it seemed incredible that they should never have met there. Perhaps if they had, Phillips mused, he would not have been so eager to leave.

"I must be going," he said, at last, rising to his feet. He reached out a hand to help her up.

"Do you really have to?" she asked.

"Professional business," he said, smiling. "But why don't you come back with me to Dras Tyghi's house? I'm sure you would be welcome."

"No—you're right. There are things I should be doing at my ship, too."

"Not preparations for leaving?" he asked anxiously.

Her eyes were radiant as she looked up at him. "I may never leave . . . now. Shall I see you again tonight?"

"Yes—I'll come here when the Lequins are at their Sunset Meeting."

"I'll look forward to that," she said.

Phillips walked back through the forest, still aware of the feel of her soft hand in his at the moment of parting. He felt a pleasant weakness that was almost like intoxication. Tonight he sensed that his dream and Carol's would merge.

Dras Tyghi, solemn faced, was waiting for him when he arrived back at the house.

"I have an apology and some explanations to make to you, my friend," said the Lequin.

As they walked together into the lounge the trained professional in Phillips emerged once more, sloughing away the romantic haziness that still lingered from his meeting with Carol.

"My group is more than ever convinced that the stimulus of intercourse between our two cultures can bring great benefits to Lequin." The alien shifted uncomfortably in his chair, staring abstractedly, as though searching for words. "What you saw yesterday afternoon was not the light-hearted game I pretended . . . but neither was it the murder you imagined."

"We're not going to get anywhere if you try to tell me that I didn't see that group of children kill another child," Phillips said. "This is fact—seen with my own eyes."

"You *thought* you saw a child," corrected Dras Tyghi. "In fact it was an *Emreth*, which had assumed the appearance of a Lequin child."

"Assumed?" Phillips frowned. "Perhaps it would help if you told me what an *Emreth* is."

"Our only species of predatory animal," Dras Tyghi said.

"One which has survived through its unique ability of adaptation. An *Emreth* has certain telepathic powers which enable it to pluck a mental image from the mind of its victim and reproduce that image in the smallest detail. Yesterday, an *Emreth* appeared as a playmate to one of the children as he was walking to join his friends. The deception was discovered when it joined the group—the child whose image it had assumed was already there, so the deception was obvious. The children took immediate action to kill the creature. *That* was what you saw."

"But if the *Emreth* had this child alone, why didn't it strike then?" asked Phillips. "It could have killed without exposing itself to the group."

"The *Emreth* doesn't *kill*," Dras Tyghi said. "Death is a by-product of its feeding. It absorbs the life force of its victim through physical contact, but a month or more may go by before the drain proves fatal."

"Then surely the victim puts up some resistance?"

Dras Tyghi shook his head. "Once the relationship is really established, the victim has no desire to resist. The absorption process produces an intense sensation of pleasure in the victim, and this ecstasy becomes more important to him than life itself."

"Then such attacks are always fatal?"

"No—luck is sometimes on the side of the victim. The contact may be broken off for some reason—the sudden interruption of another human at a crucial point, for instance, It is possible to have a brief encounter with an *Emreth* and not even be aware that one has been so close to death. In that case the victim would be left with a feeling of enervation of tiredness—symptoms which could be accounted for in other ways."

"Are there many of these things?" Phillips asked.

"Sometimes six months go by without one being detected," Dras Tyghi said. "Their numbers are dwindling gradually, in part due to counter measures, some of which have become traditional, such as the Sunset Talk Meeting. If the Recording Elder discovered one more person at the meeting than the specified number he would know that there was an *Emreth* masquerading as a member of the community. But this doesn't happen very often, because an *Emreth* would have great difficulty in maintaining its assumed form in the presence of so many minds."

"But any person who refused to attend the meeting would be suspect?" suggested Phillips.

"Exactly."

Phillips pointed to the two shining knives that hung over the fireplace. "And those?"

"Externally an *Emreth* produces a perfect image, but its internal organs are not necessarily positioned in a human manner. These knives are the best weapon with which to inflict the maximum number of wounds in the shortest possible time—increasing the possibility of hitting a mortal spot. They are kept traditionally for this purpose alone, and every family has at least one."

"And when the knife finds this mortal spot?"

"In its natural state the *Emreth* is a transparent amoeba-like creature. That is why it is so completely adaptable. When it is dead, nothing remains but a pool of quickly evaporating slime."

"The clear fluid the grass was soaked with," said Phillips. "But how do you account for the blood?"

"My little story about the *Peytru* berries didn't convince you for a moment, did it?" Dras Tyghi said. "The blood was, in fact, blood. When it is in human form, the *Emreth* can shed blood that is indistinguishable from that of a human—its reproduction of the image of a human is almost perfect."

"Then how is it possible to detect an *Emreth* at all?" asked Phillips.

"If the image is maintained, the only certain way is to kill the creature. This could lead to unfortunate accidents, if it weren't for the mysterious instinct possessed by some of our people."

"You have this instinct?"

"No—but my wife has. She has managed to escape the attentions of an *Emreth* three times in her life. Twice when she was a child, and the last time only a year ago. I killed the creature there, in the garden, next to the purple bush."

"What form had it taken?"

"In this case it assumed the shape of an old suitor of my wife—one of our rare wanderers, who left the village over ten years ago. In the case of adults, the *Emreth* often takes the form of one of the opposite sex. It's easiest prey, of course, is the lonely person."

"Yes—I can see that a lonely person would be more receptive," Phillips said thoughtfully.

Back at his ship, Phillips fed the new information into the computer. The provisional rating of Lequin as a tourist planet climbed to D minus, but the computer demanded further information on the number of *Emreth*. He had an idea that was going to be a difficult statistic to obtain. The Lequins, with their parochial society, would never have considered a planet-wide survey of such a nature in the least bit necessary.

He sat down thoughtfully with a pad and stylus and began to draw up a checklist of his needs. First on the list must be some definite way of detecting the *Emreth*. It would not be sufficient to rely on the instinct possessed by a few Lequins like Dras Tyghi's wife. Once a method of detection had been found, the next requirement was a foolproof and quick method of extermination to be carried out on a planetary scale. But TI would be unlikely to go to the expense of sending a team for such a project. Even with all its good points, they would cross Lequin off the list of probables. There were plenty of other planets in the galaxy that could be tailored to their requirements without such complications.

He pulled himself up short. The habit of being an efficient scout died hard. What did he care about TI now? His only responsibility was to live what little of life remained to him, as happily as possible. And that meant—with Carol. A surge of alarm coursed through him at the possibility of danger to her. She must be warned about the *Emreth*.

Phillips checked the ship's radio. There was no record of any incoming calls. But then the only likely caller on Lequin would be Carol, and she had not known of his existence until a few hours ago. He transmitted a call on the standard scout frequency band, then sat back and waited for acknowledgment. Carol was probably not on board her ship, but like his own, it would be equipped with the regulation robot monitor.

After ten minutes it was clear that no acknowledgment would be forthcoming. He rose to his feet, palms sweating. Carol's radio must be out of commission. That *had* to be the explanation. He could not bear to recognize the other possibility that hovered in the back of his mind like a grinning death's head. He left the ship hurriedly. There were things he had to discuss with Dras Tyghi.

The Lequin was in his garden, tending plants that grew in

a riot of coloured blossom. He looked up as Phillips approached, his face troubled.

"Have you come to any decision?"

"I make reports—not decisions," Phillips said. "But I can tell you with certainty that TI will never pass Lequin as a holiday planet."

"Then our deception was pointless."

"Believe me, Tyghi, you haven't lost a thing. What is so desirable about having this beautiful planet overrun by hordes of clumsy Earth tourists?"

"Lequin would be open to Earth knowledge, scientific techniques. . . . The stimulus would be tremendous."

"No, Tyghi. I've seen this kind of situation before. What you think would be a stimulus, would in fact be a kiss of death. Your people might accept the benefits of Earth technology, but they would make little effort to understand the processes involved."

"That is easy to say," Dras Tyghi said.

"Not at all! I repeat—you've lost nothing. You would have become totally dependent on Earth, sacrificing your present stagnation for complacent slavery. I can offer you a far greater opportunity."

Dras Tyghi frowned. "What do you mean?"

"There is a tape library on my ship, containing a comprehensive outline of Earth knowledge in every conceivable field; miles of tape, containing the basic theories produced by a thousand years of scientific civilization. I can stay here on Lequin and help your people to understand this knowledge. From there on it is up to you what you do with the knowledge, but I am sure that in the long run it will be of far more benefit to you than being presented with the fruits of Earth technology ready made."

Dras Tyghi's eyes shone. "Yes! I see what you mean, friend Phillips. My people will bless you in generations to come."

"Perhaps so—but some of *this* generation may curse me. The knowledge is there, but you will have to work hard to discover ways of applying it."

"How shall we ever repay you?" Dras Tyghi said.

"By allowing me to live here in peace on Lequin."

"You will not be returning to Earth? But surely those who sent you will send others to look for you?"

"I'm not so important, Tyghi," Phillips said. "Scouts are expendable and the galaxy is big. Somewhere in Tourism

Interplanetary headquarters a computer will take note of my disappearance and Lequin will be moved to the bottom of the list of possibly useful planets. Perhaps in another fifty or a hundred years they'll get around to trying again . . ."

Dras Tyghi embraced the Earthman, laughing. "You will receive every honour our people can give. You must come with me to the council of Elders."

"No—not yet—it would be better for you to talk to them alone. There is something else I have to do. I will meet you here after the Sunset Talk Meeting."

"As you wish, my friend," Dras Tyghi said.

"I would particularly like to hear your wife play the *Ypurr* again tonight."

Dras Tyghi smiled. "That is easily arranged."

Phillips waited until his hosts had left for the Sunset Talk Meeting, then he went into the lounge. His hands trembled as he took the shining knife down from the wall over the fireplace. He stood looking down at it for a long time, then walked out of the house to begin his walk through the shadowed forest.

Carol was waiting for him, even more beautiful than he remembered her. He stopped a few feet away from her.

"I tried to call you this afternoon," he said.

"Call me?" She looked puzzled.

"By radio. Is there something wrong with your transceiver?"

She hesitated, then: "Oh, yes . . . It blew out a couple of weeks ago. I wasn't using it here, so there didn't seem much point in fixing it."

"Scouts have been grounded for less—or don't you remember the regulations?"

"Regulations—here?" Her eyes widened at the harshness of his tone. "David—what *is* the matter?"

"I've told you—I tried to call you."

"I don't understand . . . You're different." She moved towards him.

He stepped back. His body ached to embrace her, but he avoided her, holding the knife out of sight behind him.

"Take me to your ship. I'll help you fix the radio," he said.

"No—there's plenty of time for that," Carol said.

"You mean I won't care later that there *isn't* any radio—or any ship!"

"David! You're being brutal." She was trembling. The outline of her body seemed to vibrate, becoming hazy in the dim light.

"Come back to Dras Tyghi's house with me," Phillips said. He had to fight the urge to take her in his arms with an almost physical effort. "I'd like you to meet his wife—she has a special talent that should interest you."

"David, please! Why are you hurting me like this?" she pleaded, her arms outstretched.

"Can't you guess, *Carol Remick?* I invented the way you look—but not the name. That belonged to someone else—a girl who died a long time ago, back on Earth. At first I was lonely and desperate enough to dismiss it as a coincidence, but since then I've learned some things about your kind."

"We can be happy together, here on Lequin. That's what you want, isn't it?" She moved closer.

"Get back!" he shouted, avoiding physical contact.

"I can give you happiness beyond your dreams," she whispered.

He raised his right hand, grasping the shining knife. This was what the knife was meant for. Quick, determined thrusts and this . . . thing, would be destroyed completely. There would be nothing left of this dream image . . .

"Love me," she pleaded.

She was the most beautiful thing he had ever seen. The deep brown of her eyes was the light of home on a winter night. Her face was the shining wonder of the Milky Way. Her body was the doorway to heaven. She was all hope, all life . . .

Consciousness spun like a gyroscope as the vertigo surged in on his mind. His knees gave beneath him as awareness was swept away like a cork drawn into a whirlpool.

When he opened his eyes she was bending over him. Her naked body was perfect in its loveliness, her breasts like rose tipped pearls.

"Love me," she whispered.

She flowed down into his arms. He resisted for a brief moment, then screamed in an agony of joy as the river of white fire rushed through his veins.

Spacemaster

by

JAMES H. SCHMITZ

Well-known American author, James H. Schmitz, takes two fascinating items in this new story—Man's explosive colonization of the stars and the gene structure of the human body, mixes them expertly together and comes up with a problem story written in retrospect. It might just be advisable for us to stay on Earth after all.

The dream was receding.

Haddan knew it was receding because he had insisted to himself it was a dream, a very vivid experience but untrue —a delusion which he should not attempt to retain. And he was forgetting the dream now as he woke up. There was a final memory of rain-swept greenery, long peals of thunder and then, at the very end, the sound of Auris weeping wildly nearby. For a moment, Haddan hesitated, wanting to return to her. But she was part of the delusion. . . .

He came awake.

He was sitting alone in a room, at a table which projected like a wide shelf out of the blank wall before him. The wall was of some faintly gleaming material and in it Haddan could see his own dim reflection.

His mind seemed to recoil for an instant at that point, unwilling to acknowledge the bitter reality of being on the Spacemaster ship, of having become again a prisoner of the cynical overlords and debasers of mankind. And Auris and the others with him—detected in the act of violating the basic Spacemaster law.

He should find out soon enough what the penalty was for that. It seemed very improbable that he had simply fallen asleep and escaped into dreams immediately after the capture; he must have been drugged. And now Spacemaster had brought him awake. They intended to question him, of course. He had identified himself as the leader of the group, the man responsible for the construction of the spaceship which had secretly left the City of Liot two years before. It was the truth, and his statement might make things easier for the others.

But why was he sitting here alone? Was he being watched? The table on which his hands rested was bare and of the same material as the wall, satiny to the touch. Aside from the table and his chair, the room was unfurnished. Behind him, perhaps twenty feet away, was another blank wall. To right and left, at approximately the same distance where the walls began to curve smoothly towards each other, the space between ceiling and floor was filled by curtains of curling haze through which light and colour moved in restless ripples. The stuff looked almost completely insubstantial, but Haddan realized he could not see into it. In spite of its lack of furnishing, the room gave the impression of cool elegance. And it was silent. There was not a whisper of sound except his own breathing.

They might be testing him, his nerve, his reactions. But he was gaining nothing by continuing to sit here

Haddan attempted to shift the chair back and found it immovable, attempted to get out of it and instantly felt his body grow impossibly heavy. Some trick of gravity . . . they intended him to stay where he was. He settled back into the chair, felt his normal weight gradually return.

Perhaps two minutes later, a wave of light came gliding through the section of wall before him, suddenly enough to be startling. Then the wall vanished at that point. The table at which Haddan sat now extended on without visible support beyond the partition, a flat, square slab of dull-gleaming grey material, at the other side of which, with his eyes on Haddan, sat a man in a green and red uniform.

Haddan looked back without speaking. In his lifetime he had seen only a few dozen members of Spacemaster—all the others in the City of Liot, and most of those on various occasions before he became an adult. They showed a pronounced racial similarity: stocky, strong figures and broad, heavy-boned faces with slightly tilted grey eyes. This one, whose name was Vinence, had asked Haddan a half-dozen questions in an emotionless voice when they had been taken aboard the capturing Spacemaster vessel. What happened afterwards Haddan did not remember clearly, but it seemed to him now that it couldn't have been many more minutes before he had fallen asleep. Nor could he remember what the questions had been or how he had answered them. There was no reason to doubt that the Spacemaster had used some drug on him.

Vinence appeared in no hurry to speak at the moment. He continued to study Haddan thoughtfully. Haddan let his gaze shift about the other section of the partly divided big room. It was almost a mirror image of this one; but the wall on the far side was lined from floor to ceiling with what might have been individual cabinets, and the table section before the Spacemaster was covered with rows of small coloured geometrical figures.

Vinence's flat voice asked suddenly, "What did you dream about, Haddan?"

That might not be as pointless a question as it seemed— and there was no immediate reason to be too truthful. Haddan shook his head. "I don't remember any dreams."

"I think you lie," Vinence told him after a pause, but almost as if he didn't care greatly whether Haddan was lying or not. The grey eyes retained their look of cool speculation. "There were certain records on your ship," he went on, "which you destroyed with other material when we paralysed the drive and halted the ship. Those records— I refer now to the ones dealing with the sins of Spacemaster—have since been restored. I found them interesting reading."

Haddan felt the blood drain slowly from his face. To have been caught while escaping from Spacemaster bondage might be one thing. To have planned, as he and Auris had, to provide proof of the evil Spacemaster was for human beings wherever they could be found, and to work towards Spacemaster's destruction—perhaps not in their own lifetimes or even in the next century or two, but in time— that was quite another. He did not know whether Spacemaster actually was capable of restoring material objects which had been recently destroyed; but it seemed at least possible. They knew many things they had kept their subject cities from learning. Vinence might also have gained the knowledge of the records from Auris or himself while they were drugged. It would come, Haddan thought, to much the same thing in the end.

He said nothing. He watched Vinence's tanned hand move just above the table on his right and saw a rectangle of pale light appear in the surface of the table with the motion. Vinence's eyes shifted to the lighted area and remained there for some seconds. Haddan gained the impression that the Spacemaster was reading. Then Vinence looked back at him.

"Do you happen to know," Vinence asked, "when the City of Liot was built and stationed in orbit around the Liot Sun?"

"No," Haddan said. "There were no records of that period available."

Vinence said, "The records should still be in the city, though they would be difficult to find by now. Liot was built almost three thousand years ago. It was partly destroyed a number of times in inter-city wars, but the structure remains essentially intact today . . . one of the largest cities ever to be set into space."

Liot's inhabitants, Haddan thought, had not done as well with the passing of time as their city. And for that Spacemaster must be charged.

"The treaty between Spacemaster and the Eighty-two Cities," Vinence continued, almost as if he had caught the thought, "has been in effect a little less than four centuries. Under its terms the cities engaged themselves not to build space vessels either for war or peace, and to destroy the ones they had. Spacemaster in turn assumed the responsibility of providing means of transit and trade among the cities and elsewhere as required."

"I've seen a copy of the treaty," Haddan said drily. "It didn't look like one of the cities would have signed too willingly."

Vinence nodded. "Spacemaster encountered very considerable opposition to the terms during the first few decades. Nevertheless, the terms were enforced, and opposition eventually died away. But not entirely. From time to time during the next generations some group or other would attempt to regain the means of independent space travel, either openly or furtively. The necessary measures would then be taken, and the attempt would subside.

"Of late, matters have been very quiet. Prior to the current case—yours—it had been nearly a hundred and fifty years since the construction of spacecraft was last initiated in the City of Liot. On that occasion it was also a secret action and was partly successful. One small ship was completed and was launched unobserved from the city, carrying two members of the conspiracy. They had old star charts in their possession which were to guide them to the one world in this section of our galaxy reported to have natural conditions suitable for human life without the elaborate precautions of doming. Human settlers were, in fact, supposed to have lived there in that manner during one period of the distant past.

"In spite of their lack of experience, the two travellers succeeded in reaching their goal. They returned to the City of Liot several years later with the word that there was such a planet and that human beings still existed on it, though their number was small and they had retrogressed to a condition of almost unbelievably primitive savagery. "The conspirators . . . several hundred in number . . .

now hurried through their plans to complete the construction of a ship large enough to carry them and the equipment they would need to establish the nucleus of a new human civilization on this world. In that, they did not succeed. Spacemaster got wind of the affair, and the group committed mass suicide by barricading itself in a deserted building complex in Liot and detonating a bomb which disintegrated the complex. It was falsely assumed at the time that the ship they had been building and the material they had accumulated was destroyed with them. The ship and the other items actually were sealed away in another section of the city and remained undiscovered until a few years ago.

"Which brings us to you, Haddan. . . . The manner in which you became aware of the existence of this ship and of its original purpose is not important at the moment. You did learn of these things. You banded together with other malcontents, secretly finished the construction of the ship and eventually set forth on the voyage your predecessors failed to make. And you were apprehended two years later in the process of preparing for planetfall. . . ."

Vinence paused, glanced again at the glowing rectangle in the table surface and waved his hand across it. As the light faded out, he went on, "That, I believe, is essentially the picture presented by this case. Do you agree?" His voice and expression were still impassive.

Haddan remained silent for some seconds. There was a thickness of rage in his throat which would have made it almost impossible for him to speak. In its factual details, Vinence's account of what had occurred was correct. But it was very far from complete. And it was the Spacemaster's cynical omission of the circumstances which had driven two groups of people a century and a half apart to make the same desperate effort to escape from Liot that seemed appalling. Vinence and his kind were fully aware of what had been done to the cities. It had been a deliberate, completely planned thing. Long ago, Spacemaster must have suspected a competitor for power in Liot and her sister giants in this area of space. It had isolated them from one another first, then proceeded to break them down individually. In Liot, Spacemaster had assumed control step by step, over the decades, of all the great city's functions. In Haddan's lifetime, the process had long been completed. Only Spacemaster had any understanding now even of the vast machine complexes which powered and sustained Liot; and only it retained access to the city sections where the machinery was housed. When one began to look about and check, as Haddan had done, it became clear that not even the shadow of self-government had been left.

But that was not the real crime. The crime had been committed in a much more immediate manner against the city's inhabitants . . . but so quietly that it became noticeable only when one obtained, as Haddan again had done, an understanding of the differences between the population now and that of five or six generations ago——

He told Vinence, his voice held carefully even, "I can't agree that you've presented the significant part of the picture."

"No?" Vinence said. "You believe that the emphasis should be placed on Spacemaster's misdeeds?"

Haddan looked at him, feeling the thickening in his throat again and his hands hungry to close on the throat of the unreachable man across the table. Misdeeds! When in a city, which could be calculated to have been built to contain fifteen million people, twenty thousand remained—twenty thousand at the most; more accurate figures were simply no longer available. And when the life-span average in Liot now did not appear to be even eighteen years. . . . When three out of four of the lingering descendants of the city's builders slouched past with slack-jawed, foolish faces and empty eyes——

Of what specific "misdeed" had Spacemaster been guilty there? He hadn't been able to find out; and neither—much better informed in such matters than Haddan—had Auris. They had wanted to know, to complete the record of humanity's case against Spacemaster. But too few others had been capable of giving any assistance. Whole fields of knowledge had faded from men's minds; and, in any event, that one area of knowledge might always have been Spacemaster's secret. There had not been enough time to make sure. But the condition of the people of Liot showed in itself that an enormity of some kind had been practised on them, and Haddan and Auris had corroborating evidence for that.

Vinence's voice reached Haddan again. "I was referring to the fact that the restored records contain a number of interesting speculations about Spacemaster and its activities. These records were, I believe, compiled by yourself?"

Haddan nodded. "They were."

"They were designed to be brought eventually to the attention of galactic humanity?"

Haddan hesitated, said, "Yes, that was their purpose."

The tilted cool eyes considered him for a moment. "I should like," Vinence said slowly, "to hear by what reasoning you arrived at your conclusions. I might say that nothing you tell me now could affect in any way the measures that will be taken in regard to yourself and your companions. That is a settled thing." He paused, shrugged, added almost casually. "Some of you will lose all memory of the past. The others will live out the rest of their lives without ever quite awakening again from a not too unpleasant dream. We are not inhumane, you see. We simply do what is necessary. As these measures are."

Haddan stared at him helplessly. He felt cold. He had expected death for himself, though perhaps not for the others. He had, after all, been the ringleader. Without him, none of them would have left Liot. He had tried not to think of Auris.

But this was Spacemaster's way. Not outright death, but the slow quenching of the mind, the slow decay of the body. As they had done, in a somewhat different manner, in Liot.

"You must," Vinence said, "have made certain observations. Or perhaps Dr. Auris. . . ."

Haddan, suddenly, found himself speaking. The words came out quietly, icily, though there was fury behind them. It was, of course, quite pointless. Vinence knew what had happened, and he was not a man to be ruffled by a victim's accusations. But there was some satisfaction still in letting him know that Spacemaster had not been as successful as it believed in concealing the fact that it was engaged in systematic genetic destruction.

Some came to suspect it, though by that time there was very little they could do—except to avoid for themselves such obvious traps as the marvellous automatic medical centres Spacemaster began to install throughout the city——

Vinence interrupted almost irritably. "Nearly two hundred years ago the number of capable human physicians in Liot dropped to the point where those installations became necessary, Haddan. It was only one of the many steps taken during the period of the treaty to maintain life in the cities as well as was possible."

Only one of the many steps, no doubt, Haddan agreed. But hardly with the purpose of maintaining life. Accurate records must have been difficult to find in Liot even then, but there was some reason to speculate whether it mightn't be often the strongest and most intelligent who were reported to have succumbed in the Spacemaster centres. . . .

"You think they were killed there?" Vinence said.

"Or removed from the city."

"To further weaken the strain . . . yes, I see." Vinence spoke thoughtfully, as if this were a possibility he had considered for the first time. "How did you learn about things which happened so long ago, Haddan?"

"From a message left by one of the original designers of the ship we used," Haddan said.

"You discovered this message in what way?"

Haddan said, "Not by accident. The man committed suicide with the others so that Spacemaster would not learn that the ship hadn't been destroyed. I'm his lineal descendant. He arranged to make the information about the ship available again, provided the message eventually came into the hands of somebody who could understand it. The supposition was that such a person would then also be capable of acting on the information."

"The message was coded?"

"Of course."

"I find it curious," Vinence said, "that you didn't come to our attention before this."

Haddan shrugged. "My more immediate ancestors have followed the family tradition of staying out of your medical centres. I assume that's why the strain continued as long as it did. I've also observed that tradition . . . and the other one of not applying for passage out of Liot on a Spacemaster ship."

"You feel that's another of our traps?"

"I've discovered no evidence," Haddan said, "that anyone who met the physical requirements for space flight and was accepted for passage later returned to Liot."

"I see. It appears that you were remarkably busy in a number of areas during the years before you left the city. And I suppose you formed an acquaintance with Dr. Auris in order to confirm your ancestor's suspicions about procedures in our medical centres?"

Haddan had hoped to keep Spacemaster's interest away from Auris, but the records revealed very clearly the role she had played. He said, "Yes, I obtained some additional information in that manner."

Vinence nodded. "She is another unusual member of your generation," he said. "She applied for medical training while still almost a child—the first volunteer to appear in the centres for that purpose in a decade. She wanted to help the city . . . but you know about that. She was given instruction——"

"Carefully limited instruction," Haddan said.

"Yes, carefully limited. We were making a study of Dr. Auris. It seems that on your instigation she began to study us as well. When she disappeared, it was assumed she had died somewhere in the city. Haddan, you accuse us of the genetic destruction of the space civilization of the Eighty-two Cities. What benefit do you think Spacemaster derived from the act?"

It was a question Haddan had often asked himself, and he believed he knew the answer. But there was an undefinable vague uneasiness in his mind now when he said, "The cities were threatening to dispute that space mastery of yours. At the time they were forced to accept your treaty terms, they may not have been too far away from being your equals. But you still had certain technological advantages, so you broke them first. Then, not feeling strong enough to control them indefinitely simply by forbidding them to practise space flight, you decided on a programme of deliberate, gradual extermination."

"And why," Vinence asked, "select that slow, almost interminable method? The effortless solution to such a problem would have been to open the cities to space."

"It would not have been a safe solution for Spacemaster," Haddan said, "if galactic mankind learned of the outrage." He hesitated, the sense of uneasiness stronger. For a moment, he seemed on the verge of recalling some very disturbing thing he had known once and forgotten about, and he felt sweat suddenly in the palms of his hands. Then those sensations faded. Vinence was still watching him, expression unchanged; and Haddan continued uncertainly, "You preferred to murder the cities in a manner which might, if necessary, be attributed to a natural process . . . something for which you could not be held responsible. You. . . ."

He did not see Vinence move, but with that he was suddenly plunged into complete darkness. The Spacemaster and everything else had vanished. Haddan attempted automatically to surge up out of his chair but felt intolerable heaviness dragging him back. He waited, breathing with difficulty as the heaviness eased off again, for what would happen next.

Vinence spoke then, the voice coming now out of the dark above Haddan perhaps twenty feet off and a little to his right.

"The ship is moving, Haddan. We're returning to the planet at which you were intercepted——"

And abruptly there was light.

Not the light which previously had been in the room, but the rich, bright glow of a living world swimming under its sun. All the walls of the double room, the floor and ceiling, seemed to form a single continuous window through which the brightness poured. Haddan couldn't see Vinence, but there was a blurred, greyish area up towards the right which might be an energy block behind which the Spacemaster sat. And this, Haddan thought, could very well be—it hadn't occurred to him before—the control room of the ship.

The ship was stationary in atmosphere, well down. They must have been just off the planet to have arrived here in that nearly instantaneous manner, but the manoeuvre was still one which would have been flatly impossible to the space vessel so painstakingly completed in Liot. Haddan could make out forested hills below, lush dark-green rises about which three broad rivers curved, rain clouds scudding above them. Far to the left was the hazy expanse of a sea. The area seemed to be in the tropical zone, very similar in appearance to the one where he and Auris had come down in a small boat to decide where their ship should land. As it had done then, the scene brought a sudden, almost unbearable hunger to Haddan's throat, a sense of homecoming which, for an instant, drove out everything else.

"Rather different from the parks of the City of Liot," Vinence's voice commented. "More so than you knew, Haddan. Our tests of those you had on board show that the majority would not have lived long on an undomed world. You and Dr. Auris are fortunate in that respect. Many of the others are fortunate that Spacemaster found them before they could be seriously attacked by the infections you brought back to the ship with you. . . ."

Not so fortunate, Haddan thought; otherwise the statement might be true. It was one of the incalculable risks everyone in the group had taken knowingly and willingly. They had not been able to foretell either what the impact of space-flight on genetically weakened bodies might do; and nine

men and four women of the eighty-five who left Liot died
during the first quarter of the two-year voyage. And the irony
was that they had taken such chances not knowing that
Spacemaster regarded the world towards which they were
fleeing as another of its possessions. If they had been able
to land, and enough survived, it was still unlikely they
would have escaped detection long enough to even begin to
carry out their further plans.

"And now we shall look through the instruments at what
might have been your new neighbours here," Vinence's voice
went on. "An exceptionally large troop remains as a rule
in this immediate area. . . . Yes, down at the bend in the
northern river. . . . You see the cluster of golden sparks
above the trees, Haddan? Its density indicates the presence
of the troop, each spark representing one living human being."

Haddan's glance moved up the largest of the rivers,
stopped at a firefly pattern of tiny, brilliant lights in the air on
both sides of one of the bends. They would be invisible of
course to the naked eye—a convenient method for Spacemaster to keep check on the scattered inhabitants of this
planet and, if desired, even to conduct a head count. No,
Haddan thought, he and the others from Liot couldn't have
remained undiscovered here long.

The fireflies vanished; then the scene outside the ship dark-
ened suddenly, becoming a blur of green and gold. As the
blur cleared, Haddan saw that the devices Vinence was operating had produced a close-up view of the area of the river
bend at ground level, and of fifty or sixty of the human
"troop". It was a convincing illusion—he might have been sitting among them—and more than a view. His ears recorded
a babble of shrill calls from a group of children at the
edge of the water; two women were shouting back and
forth across the river. After a few seconds, Haddan realized
there were also tactile sensations . . . a sense of warmth,
of moving air; and, very faintly, odours of vegetation and
water.

His gaze shifted about the group. They were not, he
thought, remarkably handsome people, though there was a
great deal of individual variance in that. All—even the bath-
ing children—looked dirty; almost all were naked. They appeared to be chiefly engaged in grubbing around in reeds and
thickets for edible substances, vegetable and animal. Only
a few of the faces nearest him gave the impression of cal-

culating intelligence. But there was, with very few exceptions, an air of alertness and robust energy about them which no group of corresponding size in Liot would have suggested. And the number of both grizzled oldsters and small children was startling. There had been *no* healthy old people in Liot.

It was a group which could have been retaught many things long forgotten here, Haddan thought, and which should have learned them quickly. The plan had not been a hopeless one in that respect; the possibility of developing a new civilization on this world had existed. And that made it the more strange that no civilization did exist here, that the descendants of the old-time settlers had regressed instead to this manner of living . . . almost exactly, except for the dexterous use of pieces of wood and rock in their varied pursuit of meals, the manner of a troop of animals. Vinence might have used the term contemptuously; but it was a correct one.

Spacemaster's work again? It very easily might be, Haddan decided, and it probably was. Why else should there be so *few* of these people on a world which obviously could have supported a far denser human population—even one which had lost every scrap of technological understanding. Yes, Spacemaster, almost certainly. A somewhat different form of degradation here, perhaps brought about for an entirely different purpose. But it had been done deliberately——

"Galactic humanity," Vinence's voice said from above him. "You're looking at a part of it here, you know, Haddan! As large a part, as a matter of fact, as you're likely to find in any one place on this world . . . and studying them at close range now, do you think Spacemaster would be really concerned about anything you could tell these people? It might be interesting to watch you trying to describe the City of Liot to them in the vocabulary of grunts which their use of speech amounts to.

"But, of course, you knew that. You understood it would take generations to bring about any significant change here, and that you and your companions could only begin the process. But this is one small, badly stunted twig on the great tree of mankind. You were planning to get word to the others. The number of them alone would make them unconquerable now. Only fourteen thousand years ago, they were still confined to a single planet not very different from this one. But then they drove out into the galaxy, established great civilizations on a thousand new worlds, scattered the self-sustaining giant cities through space. . . . *That's* the humanity Spacemaster would have to fear, isn't it, if it learned what we did to the Eighty-two Cities?"

"Or," Haddan said, "if it learned what you've done to this world! That alone would damn you—and in the end it will. You won't escape mankind's judgment for ever."

There was silence for some seconds, even the muted sounds of human activity at the river dwindling into nothing. Then Vinence spoke again.

"There's a very curious fact here, Haddan. You—and you're far from unique in it—have hypnotized yourself into believing certain facts about Spacemaster. By doing it, you were able to ignore another possible explanation for the way things have gone in Liot, though there are indications that it has never been very far from your awareness. Perhaps one can't blame you for the continuous self-deception, but it must end now. And I think that essentially you do want to know the true reason for what will be done with you and your friends."

The words seemed to just miss making sense. A queer, sharp surge of panic began to arise in Haddan. He heard himself blurt out thickly, "What are you talking about?"

There was no answer. Instead, complete darkness closed about him again. Haddan waited, his thoughts whirling, shifting drunkenly as if in shock. What *had* Vinence just said? He seemed unable to remember it clearly. What self-deception?

He realized that Vinence was speaking again.

"It took two years to cover the distance between Liot and the world we just left," the voice said. "But we are not called Spacemaster for nothing, so don't be too surprised now. What you will see is as real as it appears."

The thick darkness was lifting from the double room as he spoke, and through the surrounding endless window of walls and ceiling and floor the stars of space shone in. On Haddan's left was the harsh yellow-white glare of a nearby sun; and dead ahead, reflecting the glare like a blazing jewel, were the faceted walls of Liot. He recognized the city instantly, though he had seen this outside view before only in the instant after a long unused small lock opened to let out their ship. Then the drive immediately had hurled them away from the Liot Sun with almost the speed of light.

The city blurred now, reshaped itself, closer. The Spacemaster ship was gliding in towards a huge opened entry lock. Another blur, and it hung in the lock's mouth.

"What do you see, Haddan?"

He stared down the brilliantly lit, starkly empty lock. At the far end, a mile away, was another vast, gaping circle. Beyond it, more light. . . .

The thought came suddenly, numbing as death:

"The city is empty!"

Haddan didn't know he had said it. But he heard Vinence reply.

"Yes, empty . . . open to space. Liot was the last of the Eighty-two. It's been lifeless for nearly a year. And now"— the voice was flat and expressionless again—"we'll go to the worlds and cities of the galactic mankind on which you based your hopes. I think you've begun to understand consciously what we will find there."

And, in that instant, he had.

Perhaps only hours later, Haddan stood at a window of a great globular structure floating less than half a mile above the surface of a world called Clell. A sense of heavy, almost paralysing physical shock hadn't yet drained completely from his body. But his thoughts were clear again.

He had seen the dead worlds, the dead space cities of galactic mankind—enough of them; too many. Clell still lived, in a fashion. The glassy roofs of the flat, wide buildings stretching towards the horizon across the pleasant plain below Haddan sheltered eighty thousand human beings . . . the greater part of what was left of the proud species of Man. Clell was the next to last world he would see, and the last he would see while he still retained the knowledge of who and what he was.

Spacemaster's plans for his personal future in themselves were not distressing. They would take away his memories, but he would be living on the green world far away from Clell where there was thunder and rain, perhaps as a member of the band he had watched on the river's banks—not the most handsome of people on the whole, and somewhat soiled, but not unhappy. In Vinence's phrasing, he would have become a neoprimitive, one tiny, temporary, individual factor in Spacemaster's gigantic, centuries-spanning plan to obtain survival for the human race. And Auris would be there, though Haddan wouldn't be able to remember her, or she him. He recalled his feelings when he had looked down on that world and during the few hours he walked about on it, and he knew the other Haddan would be contented enough in his new existence. He certainly preferred that prospect to the drugged, comforting fantasies which would be the final life experience of the human majority on Clell . . . the majority which could not be employed in the plan.

But it was not what he wanted. And the immediate question was how far Spacemaster could be trusted.

Haddan's gaze shifted back to the table behind him. It was littered with maps, charts, masses of other informative material, much of it incomprehensible. But, added to what he had been shown from Vinence's incredible ship, there had been enough he understood to present the story of the genetic collapse of Man—or Spacemaster's version of it.

It was not too implausible. The death seed of multitudinous abnormal genes had been planted in the race before it set out to explore and inhabit the galaxy, and with the expansion their rate of development increased. For another long time, improving medical skills maintained the appearance of a balance; it had become very much less easy for civilized Man to die even under a heavy genetic burden. But since he continued to give short shrift to any government audacious enough to make the attempt of regulating his breeding preferences, that burden also continued to grow.

A point regularly came where medical knowledge, great as it might be, was suddenly shown to be no longer capable of the human repair work needed now to keep some specific civilization on its feet. The lethal genes, the innumerable minor mutations, had established at last a subnormal population, chronically sick and beginning to decrease rapidly in numbers. Spacemaster's charts indicated that this period, once entered, was not prolonged. When there were simply not enough healthy minds and bodies left to attend to the requirements of existence, the final descent became catastrophically swift and was irreversible. On Liot, Haddan had been living through the last years of such a period, modified only by Spacemaster's intervention.

Spacemaster, with its supermachines and superscience, had come into existence as an organization almost too late to act as more than humanity's undertakers. Liot had been the last of all islands of galactic civilization. In less than fifteen centuries, the race had gone everywhere from its peak of achievement and expansion to near-extinction. Spacemaster

believed it could still be rebuilt from its remnants, but that
the rebuilding required surgical ruthlessness and long-contin-
ued supervision.

That was the story Haddan had been given . . . and why, he
thought, should they bother to lie to him? But there were
puzzling features, and questions left unanswered. What was
Spacemaster? Some superior genetic strain which had possessed the self-discipline and foresight to eliminate any
threatening weaknesses in its ranks and to remain apart from
deteriorated groups? Then why should they have undertaken the stupendous task of attempting to recreate the human race from the survivors of the foundering civilizations?
They themselves, at an incomparable level of technological
achievement, were the new humanity.

The reflection had raised eerie possibilities. There was
the fact that he found it impossible to feel at ease in Vinence's presence. Something in the Spacemaster's appearance,
the manner in which he moved, sent constant alert signals to
Haddan's brain . . . a difference there, not too obvious but
profoundly disturbing. It was as if his senses would not accept that Vinence was another human being, and the thought
had come that perhaps on one of the dying worlds a race
of robots had been brought into existence and given the
task of saving mankind—that Vinence and his fellows were
still attempting to carry out the task, with mechanical per-
severance, mechanical lack of real interest and, actually, without too much intelligence.

Because Spacemaster's plan . . . or as much of it as Haddan
had been allowed to see . . . contained obvious elements of
sheer, senseless futility. . . .

Or Vinence might be, if not a robot, a member of a genuine alien species, one masquerading as human beings, and
with very different designs on the survivors of humanity
than Haddan had been told. There was the world Tayun to
which he and Auris and such others of the Liot group as would
not be retained on Clell were destined to go. It would be the
last group Spacemaster could add to its sparse human breeding stock on Tayun. It had kept the City of Liot functioning
for a year after Haddan's departure. Then it became obvious
that there would be no more viable births in the city, that
the last drop of genetic usefulness had been drained from
the shrunken population. The survivors were transferred to
Clell, and the city left open to space but intact . . . because

eventually human beings should return to lay claim to it
again.

That, Vinence said, was Spacemaster's purpose. For centuries it had drawn those who still seemed sufficiently sound
out of the subnormal groups under its attention and moved
them to Tayun, which of all known worlds came closest to
matching the conditions which had existed on primitive
Earth. Not too easy a world for human beings to live on without the tools and conveniences of civilization, and not too
difficult. Which was exactly as it should be for Spacemaster's
purpose. Tayun was the laboratory in which, over the course
of generations, any concealed inherited weaknesses were to
be worked very thoroughly out of the transplanted human
strains. Throughout the long probationary period, they were
therefore to have only their natural endowment to see them
through the problems they encountered. This was the reason
that transferred adults were not allowed to retain the memories of their previous life. Haddan, Auris and the rest
would be left in the vicinity of some large group which
could be counted on not to take too unamiable an attitude
towards befuddled strangers. Since they were physically and
mentally well above the present average on Tayun, it should
not take them long to overcome their initial handicaps among
the group's members. If their memories were left intact, it
would be too difficult for them to avoid the temptation of
introducing minor innovations to make life more easy for
themselves and the others.

"It isn't intended that life should become more easy there
for quite a few centuries," Vinence said, "except as the strain
improves its natural ability to meet the conditions around
it. . . ."

He acknowledged that for a while it had appeared that the
Spacemaster experiment on Tayun was too drastic and
would fail. Diseases, shifts of climate, animal enemies, and
their own latent genetic liabilities seemed to be killing the
"neoprimitives" off faster than they could be brought in. But
during the past sixty years, their number had first stabilized,
and then had begun to increase detectably. The first crisis
was over.

It all looked quite logical, so far. Haddan knew little of
genetics as Spacemaster understood it; it had been among
Liot's "lost" sciences. He was willing to accept that there
were no effective gentler alternatives to letting a species

cleanse itself in a world-wide natural framework of the individuals who lacked essential qualifications to survive. And having seen the neoprimitives of Tayun for himself, he had not been greatly surprised by Vinence's explanation.

But the further steps of Spacemaster's plan were—when one stopped to give them any thought at all—completely and unbelievably insane. . . .

Hearing a door open and close behind him, Haddan turned and saw Vinence come across the room.

He stood silently, watching the stocky, strong-looking figure, the bland, impassive face with the tilted grey eyes. Every Spacemaster he had seen so far looked very much like Vinence. What *was* the wrongness about them? He couldn't have said exactly. Perhaps it was a hint of unevenness in the motion, the suggestion of a marionette propelled along by expert hands holding invisible strings. The smooth features and coolly calculating eyes . . . was this a robot? Haddan felt aversion, the concealed ripple of horror, crawl again over his skin.

Vinence stopped at the other side of the table, glancing at the materials scattered about it. He pulled out a chair and sat down.

"Did you get much out of this?" he asked Haddan.

"Not too much."

"It's a large subject," Vinence acknowledged. He stared thoughtfully at Haddan, added, "Our business on Clell has been concluded. Besides Dr. Auris and yourself, four of your group chose Tayun. The others will remain here."

Haddan said incredulously, "Only four preferred Tayun?"

Vinence shurgged. "That's a very high average, Haddan. I did not expect so many. In the terminal generations of a culture like Liot almost nothing is left of the motivation to survive as a species. There were three of you of whom we felt nearly certain; but the majority of your group were intellectual rebels who faced the risks of leaving Liot without undue qualms largely because they have always been a little detached from living realities. For them there could be no compensation in beginning life again as a memoryless savage. The dreams of Clell held much more interest."

He added, "There was a time when Spacemaster might have taken another dozen from that particular group for Tayun, without their consent. The tests rate at least that many as qualified. But no combination of tests shows every essential. We learned that when we went only by them and our own judgment, and nothing else, we ended almost invariably by having weakened the Tayun strain."

"And what," Haddan asked, "are you going to accomplish finally by strengthening it?"

Something flickered for an instant in the Spacemaster's eyes. Then his expression changed slowly, became mocking, watchful, perhaps menacing; and the certainty grew in Haddan that his question had not come as a surprise.

Vinence said, "That is a curious thing to ask at this late moment." He nodded at the table before him. "Are you disagreeing with some of the conclusions you found there?"

Haddan looked at him. Why argue really? He would not change Spacemaster's plans . . . except perhaps unfavourably as regards to himself. Vinence's attitude of expectancy suggested he might be on the verge of entering a prepared trap. His reaction to the information allowed him, to the things he had been shown and told—without apparent good reason so far—could be the factor which determined what they did in his case. And it was quite possible that they preferred to exclude too questioning an attitude from man's new genetic pattern.

Why not accept Tayun? For him as an entity, there certainly would be compensations for becoming absorbed by the living racial strain. At the very least, it was better than to spend the rest of his days in the sterile dream-halls of Clell——

He heard himself say, "It was a logical question. The charts show what you've told me. Eventually Tayun Man is to be allowed to develop his own civilization. During that period, he should be a trifle hardier physically, a trifle more mentally competent, than the species was perhaps twenty thousand years ago. Serious genetic defects will have been burned out. But in every essential it will be the same species. Spacemaster will have provided mankind with a fresh start. That's what it amounts to, isn't it?"

Vinence nodded. "Very nearly."

Haddan said "Your helpfulness does go a little further, of course. The redevelopment of civilization when it begins will not be haphazard. Man will automatically come across prepared information in some concealed form or other at the moment he can best put it to use. So this second time he should advance very rapidly. But will some super-organization like Spacemaster still be in control of him then?"

"Hardly," Vinence said. "And not at all after they begin to spread through the galaxy again. That would be not only undersirable but impossible. We've learned that much."

"Then it seems," Haddan said, "that Spacemaster is committing an act of lunacy. If there's to be nothing but a fresh start, the whole cycle should be repeating itself a few thousand years from now. They'll have made the same mistakes and again be well advanced in the process of self-destruction. There's no reason to expect anything else—and of course you're aware of that. But unless you already know how to keep it from occurring . . ."

Vinence shook his head. "We don't." He hesitated. "There is a vast difference between restoring the health of a species and attempting to change its natural attitudes in any significant manner. The last is an enormously complex process which contains a much greater likelihood of doing harm than good. I'm engaged myself in Spacemaster's investigations of possible means to prevent renewed racial suicide, and have been for a long time. We are not at all certain that even a theoretical solution can be found." The tone was bland, the grey eyes still fixed unblinkingly on Haddan.

Haddan said doggedly, "A solution will have to be found, or the plan is almost meaningless. And until it is found, Spacemaster is wasting anyone like Dr. Auris or myself on Tayun . . . anyone capable of independent abstract thinking, which certainly isn't a vital requirement in Tayun Man at present. The strain can get along without our kind for a while. You should be putting every functioning mind you can reach to use in looking for the answers you don't have. That should be our assignment in Spacemaster's plan. Anything else is indefensible."

Vinence was silent for some moments. Then he shrugged, said, "There is one thing wrong with that assumption, Haddan. I mentioned that there are complexities in such a project. They are much greater than you realize. Certainly neither you nor Dr. Auris are stupid—but your individual remaining life expectancies are less than fifty years. You would be dead before you could learn half of what you would need to know to begin to be useful to us in such work. There is simply too much to be understood."

Haddan stared at him. "But you were capable of understanding it?"

"Yes, I was."

"Then what——"

Haddan's voice died in his throat. Vinence had raised his hands to his face, cupping the sides of his jaw in his palms, fingers pressed vertically along the cheeks. The hands seemed to make a slight tugging motion; then they lifted the Spacemaster's head from the sturdy neck and placed it un-hurriedly upright on the table, a little to one side.

Haddan felt incapable of breathing or moving. He stared in a fascination of repugnance at the head, at the eyes—still fixed on him—at the grey, glistening, jellylike surface of the sectioned neck. Then the head's mouth moved.

"The Spacemaster's body," Vinence's voice said, with no change in tone or inflection—it seemed to be still coming out of the head—"is an interesting biological machine, Had-dan. As a matter of fact, it represents a partial solution to the problem we were discussing, though not a very satis-factory one. There are pronounced disadvantages. This body, for example, couldn't exist for minutes if exposed to the open air of even so gentle a world as Clell. If you hap-pened to touch me, I would die almost at once. And if you hadn't been enclosed in a screen of filtering energies since the instant we met, there would have been the same regret-table result. The 'Spacemasters' you may have seen in the City of Liot were manipulated automatons—displayed oc-casionally to produce some specific effect on the population. A Spacemaster body can tolerate very few of the realities of life as you know them. It experiences almost everything through instruments, at second hand. It uses no food, can-not sleep, cannot reproduce its kind.

"But we are human, and have had wholly human bodies. What you see is the result of a fusion with something which is nearly, but not quite, another form of life, and with the non-living instrumentation which allows us to move, see, sustain normal gravity and—as you notice—to speak at con-siderable length. Nevertheless, we remember what human realities were like, and at times we miss them excruciatingly. We experience remorse, frustration, the sense of failure; and we are often too vividly aware of the artificial mon-strosities we have become. As I said, there are disadvantages to this kind of living.

"The other side of the matter is that the Spacemaster body lives for a very long while, though eventually it does wear out along with its human component. So there's time to learn and understand some of those very complicated matters one must know in order to do what is necessary . . . which is what Spacemaster has been doing for the past two thousand years."

Hadden said hoarsely, "How long have you . . ."

"Not quite half that period. It was roughly nine hundred years ago that I faced the same choice as you do today. I'm a little shopworn by now, though it hardly shows yet."

Vinence's hands reached down, lifted the head, replaced it on the neck, twisted deftly, quickly and withdrew. "This may seem an overly dramatic demonstration," the Spacemaster went on, "but it has its uses. More than one apparent candidate has lost all interest in further discussion around this point."

Hadden drew in a deep breath, asked, "You're offering me a body of that kind?"

"Why else would we be talking about it?"

Something stirred in the back of Hadden's mind—a soft confusion of light and colour, whispering rain, and Auris's sweetly intelligent face. Then it all faded.

He said, "I accept, of course."

"Of course you do," Vinence agreed. "There's been almost no question of that. But we've learned to wait until a potential recruit sees the need for membership and demands it, as his right, before we reveal the conditions. In the past, too many who were persuaded to become Spacemasters on the basis of our judgment of their qualifications eventually found it was a burden they no longer wanted to carry. And it's so very easy for any of us to step out on a pleasant planet, and breathe its air and die.

"But you've made your choice. We won't lose you. Neither are we afraid of losing Dr. Auris, who made the same decisions some hours before you."

In spite of everything, that came as a shock. After a moment, Hadden asked, "Then when . . . do we begin?"

Vinence said, "There are no formalities. You'll be inoculated at once. There will be a few uncomfortable months then until the fusion is complete. But afterwards . . . we build better bodies now than this one of mine . . . you should both have a full twelve hundred years ahead of you to work on Spacemaster's great problem, and Man's. And who knows? That may be the period in which the answer is finally found."